Heart Strings of Steele

Laticia Waggoner

ISBN: 1979741352

ISBN-13: 978-1979741354

Dedication

To my three children and their beautiful families. Travis, Casey, and Johnna. Thank you for your love, and never ending support. You and your families are God's gift to me that make my world so complete. Thank you also, for the use of your names in this fictitious story……

Acknowledgments

Tyler Erickson thank you for your many hours of hard work creating my book cover, front to back, for being the final editor of the story in this first book of the Steele series, also for being like a third son to me. Lindy Cosper thank you for being my sounding board editor on this roller coaster book ride, along with helping give my novel the perfect title. A shout out to Mr Shawn Carroll for his generosity of a final read before going to print. To the community of Bisbee Arizona for always being in my heart. There could not have been a better place to have as the stage for this story to be born and blossom.

Prologue

Even from across the street I could see her quiver when he touched her shoulder to let her know he had arrived for what looks to be a breakfast rendezvous. As he settles in at the table I think to myself how absurd it is to have such an intense emotional reaction to someone at a mere touch. Who am I kidding … I know exactly what that's like, but it's still absurd. Their unmistakable chemistry makes it difficult to turn away. I'm happy for them. Or am I jealous. Perhaps I'm just sad. I push the self-pity out of my head when I notice her demeanor change. Anger? I see him shrugging and shaking his head in what I can only assume is his attempt to dismiss whatever the woman reacted to. This is personal. I should look away. I can't. It's not the spectacle, but whatever is at stake for these two I feel somehow that it will affect me. I am rooting for her. No … them. They start yelling. Now more people are looking. The growing audience's uncomfortable glances are trying to convince the arguing couple to find a new venue. I am only concerned. How could something so beautiful transform so quickly into something so ugly. It occurs to me that it hadn't transformed, it had always been both. The thought scares me, but then I realize something and I calm down. The couple soon storms off in opposite directions. I eventually return to my tea and my concerned face melts into a satisfied smile. I love this town.

Chapter One

I sit enjoying a warm Sunday morning in Bisbee on the long veranda of the Copper Queen Café and Saloon, having my usual hot tea and toast. Being the forevermore romantic, that I am, I always start my Sunday's here, doing a little people watching and reminiscing about the earlier years growing up here with my family. Then I plan my week at the Brickstone Antique & Art Gallery, that I opened late last fall just before Thanksgiving when I came back home to Bisbee. I found it easy to feel right at home again when I came back. It was not long after coming back that I started this Sunday ritual on my only day off. Before long I also, found myself settling into a pattern of other daily routines: early morning walks to and back from the City Park where I discovered that my activities coincided with the daily rituals of certain other people. No matter that our life paths never cross other than on this hour and place. There is always the old hippie gentleman that has probably never left Bisbee. He is always dressed in army-surplus clothing, with long braided hair down his back, a greying beard down to mid chest, still rejecting established social customs, and with his handwritten cardboard sign continues to stand his ground on opposing violence and war. The music coming from his guitar is still as sweet to my ears as it was in the early seventies. Then there is the pretty Mexican woman with the beautiful skin and dark hair that jogs this path every morning with her black Scottish terrier named MacTavish. MacTavish stays in the exact rhythm with her until he hears the music that makes him dart towards the hippie playing the guitar for only a few moments before he will double back, and fall into the jogging rhythm again with his owner whose name I have discovered is Laura Pilner. Also, on Mondays and Wednesdays there is a stretch yoga class of about six to eight ladies with their colored mats spread out on the concrete. Our very influential Mayor is also, just a few steps ahead of me every morning, his steps are a steady quick pace, so I like to keep pace with his steps if I can without feeling like a stalker. I find that this early morning ritual gives me a good feeling before starting my day at the Brickstone. This means I have at least said good morning to people that I may not know personally, or see any other time in my day, but they are a constant in my life that I believe to be good people that make up part of the culture here. After my days are done at the Brickstone, I find that I like to unwind my day with some light yoga, and then either a Chakra or sound meditation. My Gallery is in the heart of the community on the east side of Tombstone Canyon in an old historic brick building that has been vacant for a better part of the decade. With a jewelry store on one side, that has many designs of unique jewelry done with "Bisbee Blue Turquoise," then on the other side there is a quaint coffee shop where you can purchase a cup of coffee from your choice of beans that have been imported from different places all over the world just to satisfy your personal taste in coffee. My building was built sometime in 1883. The traffic flow is constant up and down Tombstone Canyon, as anyone that knows Bisbee is aware, and this makes the exposure to the Brickstone perfect.

My store front has two very large original picture windows on each side of the original double doors that are heavily carved of quarter sawn oak with full length beveled oval leaded glass windows in each of them. I fell in love with the building from the moment that I laid eyes on those doors. The handles are heavy vintage ornate brass with lots of Victorian scrolling, just what one would expect for a Bisbee Gallery.

Sitting here on this veranda, I realize that this may just be my favorite place in all of Bisbee. It still has that same flavor of the stylish historic old west ambiance that I have always loved so much. It is part of the Copper Queen Hotel that was built, in 1902, by Phelps Dodge Mining Company as a place for dignitaries and investors to relax in luxury. It was designed in the classical Italianate style with some of the fixtures and trim still being original. The interior is furnished with expensive hardwoods and California Redwood trim, hand carved wood pillars, imported Italian Marble blanketing the main lobby areas, and one-of-a kind Tiffany fixtures. It has such a feel of romance to me, maybe because growing up here I spent a lot of time sitting on a bench across the street with my best friend Joseph Dalecki. We would set on that bench watching people coming and going. We would create their stories, who they might be, where they were from, and why they were at the, believed to be haunted, Copper Queen Hotel in Bisbee Arizona.

Joseph Dalecki, of course this man would again today find his way into my thoughts. This is almost a daily occurrence usually brought on by all the memories of he and I that surround me in this small quirky town that I choose to call home once again. The story of Joseph, or Joey as I have always called him is mystifying to me. No matter what I did after I left Bisbee, or no matter who I dated I was never able to get over the so called boy next door, my best friend. You see not only did I come home because I had a dream to open up my own Art and Antiques Gallery here, but I hoped that Joey would feel the same magnetic pull that

I have felt for the past several years regarding us, and find his way back to Bisbee, and me. The thing is we sort of made this unwritten promise to each other way back when. We promised that we would both come back to Bisbee one day, because after all this is where our hearts would always be. Of course there is a big possibility that he has no idea that I have made true to that promise, and have moved back. Also, this promise was made way before I knew, or at least could admit that he was the one that I would be in love with all of my life. I know that promises made by young hearts are not always going to be kept. Life is just more complicated when you grow up. Joey with intention or not has kept his life very private and away from me, and everyone else in Bisbee as far as I can tell. I have not heard from him in seven years. His parents still live in the family Manor here, and he has a brother and family that live here as well. I also, have had very little contact with any of them since I have been back, other than church at St. Patrick's the few times I have gone.

I have actually socialized very little since I have been here and opened my Gallery, other than time spent with my dear girlfriend Myranda Rain. It seems that most of my time is spent trying to make the Gallery a success along with all of the other fun shops, and galleries in Tombstone Canyon. When I am not at the Brickstone, I am usually on a buying trip so that I always have new art pieces and collectibles in so that I can keep all of the locals as well as the tourists coming back. At night I have kept myself busy reading and learning about the rich history of Bisbee. Somehow this wonderful history all escaped me as I was growing up here. Now that I have come back as an adult with a business interest of my own, I find that I am fascinated by the incredible history.

There is not only the history of this hotel that intrigues me, or anyone else visiting Bisbee, but I now know that people come here from all over the country to purchase the beautiful Turquoise that was mined here. Our Turquoise is most well-known for its deep blue color. Also, famous from only the Bisbee Mine is the Turquoise with chocolate brown matrix, and red webbed matrix.

The intrigue of Bisbee could go on forever. It was founded in 1880, as was one of the richest mineral sites in the world. Producing Gold, Silver, Copper, Lead, Zinc, and Turquoise. Bisbee also, by the early 1900's due to the booming mining industry, had become the largest city between St. Louis and San Francisco. Population of twenty thousand by the beginning of the century. Today the population is somewhere between six and seven thousand. It was then one of the most cultured cities in the west. The town today is still home to the nation's oldest baseball field, called the Warren Ball Park. The state's oldest golf course, known as Turquoise Valley, and the state's first community library, the Copper Queen Library, are all still in current operation today, to the public.

Then there is the notorious "Brewery Gulch," from back in the day with its many saloons and brothels. In its heyday the gulch boasted nearly 50 saloons, and was considered to be one of the liveliest spots in the west. Historic taverns still remain, with the rich character and boom-town flavor of yesteryear.

Today of course most of the mining has come to an end. Our quaint community is now slowly becoming known for its small town charm, eccentric character, and picturesque mountain side homes that is a stone's throw from Mexico. Colorful turn-of-the-nineteenth-century Victorian-style buildings, that have been resurrected to become an eclectic mix of galleries, boutiques, eateries, bars, and B&BS. There is, more than ever, a free spirited culture that accentuates the vibe of an ever growing art and music community.

All of this is set in Southern Arizona Cochise County, part of the beautiful desert Mule Mountains. The county received its name from the great Apache Indian Chief Cochise, who settled and lived in many parts of the county mountain ranges of the Chiricahua's, Dos Cabezas, Dragoon's, and the Huachuca's.

Now this morning thinking of all of these things as I sit here drinking my tea in this particular place that is so dear to my heart, I realize that there is always these intimate thoughts that I cannot ever seem to escape. Sometimes I think of my past as a mystery unsolved, a romance unfulfilled. I feel somehow that the time and place for real love has been omitted from the script of my life.

I knew even when I was only eleven and seeing Joseph Dalecki for the first time, that this boy flying past third base was part of my destiny. Can an eleven year old fall in love? I only know that I have never had a more heart stopping moment.

Chapter Two

Myranda Rain had hardly had time to sit the next day, at the El Charro Restaurant, where we were to have lunch before I just blurt out, do you think that Joseph Dalecki will ever come back to join his family business?

She gives me this look with those serious eyes in only the way that my dear aristocratic friend Myranda can.

She says, well I have never really had any reason to think about it until now. I did hear that he has a big career with the FBI in Washington DC, so law is a career that I never thought of Joey Dalecki going into. His spirit was always too wild and crazy. But, that means he probably is not coming back here to live anytime soon. Pax did you ever see or talk to him after you left Bisbee?

Yes, once or twice while we were both still in college we connected by telephone a couple of times just to say hi, and I guess maybe to see how life was going for the other. The last time we spoke he shared with me that he was involved with someone there at the University, and he thought that he loved her. That was seven years ago. After that I guess we were both just busy with our lives, and we lost contact. However, I always thought that we would both end up coming back here to live

one day. We both talked about it all of the time. Of course we used to talk about a lot of things regarding our dreams when we would be playing catch at the Vista Park, sitting in my back yard, or on one of our long day hikes in the Huachuca deserts. He always said his heart was right here at home, so his plan was to come back to live permanently, and make his living here after he was done with school in Tempe. He also, talked about doing some traveling through Mexico, and Central America before he returned to settle down. When I finished school, I also, did some traveling to places like Panama City, Belize, and Costa Rica. I never really admitted this to myself, or anyone else, but. I secretly always hoped that by some coincidence Joey and I would run in to each other. You know kind of a serendipity thing.

Pax you always were and still are the romantic one. I will never understand why you two never got together romantically before he left for College. Until then you were inseparable. Everyone could see you were in love, even though you both tried so hard to deny it. Think about all of the problems that your just friends, friendship caused when you tried to date other people. Talk about drama, I remember that I was always the one, as your best friend, stuck trying to convince all of your dates, and boyfriends that your relationship with Joey was more like a brother-sister kind of thing. Yeah-right I hardly believed it myself. I do remember that you shared with, me more than once back then, that he had this do not get any closer persona to him, even with you. So probably the two of you never crossed that line, with good reason. He seemed to have deep seeded demons of some type that made him the ultimate hard core party boy.

Myranda, it has now been so long since I've seen, or talked to him that this image that I hold onto is probably no longer real. It makes my heart feel good to know that he took full advantage of his baseball scholarship opportunity, at ASU, to receive his education. I always thought that he would drop out of school to go pro. I know that he had some offers to do so, but doing that with his love of partying, and no commitment life style, could have led to disaster. Though back then I also, felt the sexy baseball professional athlete persona fit his playboy party life style more than anything else. Well maybe not I also, always felt that he partied just to escape something in his home life that he had buried way down deep in his soul where no one could see it. Even I never got close enough to him that I could understand what was hidden in his soul. I believe growing up there was no one that I ever knew that was any closer as friends than he and I, but there were always things about him that a good friend just knew to leave alone. He had what seemed like a perfect family, money, good looks, friends, and was the hometown high school baseball star. So I never could completely wrap my mind around the reasons that I felt so uneasy about his home life, and his family. Even today I sense that there are truly few people, in this small community, that know the story of the powerful Dalecki's. It is like those large black iron gates, and tall walls that are to protect, not only their privacy, but some deep family secrets. There has always been a great deal of mystery that surrounds them. I have always wondered what really goes on most of the time behind those enormous doors of the family Dalecki Manor up there high on "Snob Mountain". As we used to refer to it way back when, I say laughing.

Pax, I know what you mean, that manor looks so intimidating

to me, and other than Joey, I never felt that his family was very friendly.

Joey's mom, Charlotte, came into the Brickstone, not long ago, right after my grand opening, to say hello, and to look around. She mentioned that the manor needed some up-dated changes in décor, and that she might call on me one day to come over to give her some suggestions regarding a few art pieces. She thought that some new art on the walls might be just what she was looking for, along with the renovations that they are in the process of doing. When I asked her about Joey, she was so vague about what he is doing, that I got the feeling they do not talk very often. She said his job keeps him traveling all the time so he rarely gets back home for visits. They were always so close, but for whatever reason she was not comfortable talking about him, so I did not ask many questions. I did get out of her though that he never married.

Pax, tell me the truth is Joey the reason you never found the perfect man to spend your life with?

I feel myself biting my bottom lip as I always do when I am nervous about something. To be honest, maybe he is I say. I just know that I think about him constantly now that I am back, and always wondering what I would do, or how I would react, if one day he walked through the Brickstone doors with that one of a kind swagger that only he has. I think maybe I am just now realizing that I was in love with him the entire time back then, or maybe it is just all of the memories of he and I that surround me each day now that I am back in Bisbee. However, I have always seemed to compare every guy that I have ever dated with him. Then I always managed to end up alone. It has always been impossible for me to forget about Joey. His long and lanky build, his black hair that always strayed below his collar with just enough curl to it. Those narrow hollow cheeks that always had the scruff of a five-o-clock shadow, even in high school. He always had that kind of swagger that only a boy or man of great confidence has.

Paxy, I do believe you may be giving yourself a fever just talking about that tall drink of water, hunk of a meat, Joey.

Myranda you're not far from wrong about that. I get such a feeling in my heart, which goes soul deep, when I think of him even after all this time. Of course there is something else too, even if I never see him again. As we have been talking I realize that the curious spirited, and daring side of me wants to have the chance to break through that complex privacy, and solve the puzzle of the mystifying Joey Dalecki, and his family, that I never had the chance to do years ago.

Growing up I always wanted to know more about his family, but for some reason he never really talked about them, or let anyone get too close to them, or his home life. I was only at the manor a few times in all those years. I remember it being so daunting with those enormous shining luster black twelve foot double doors with that big Griffin Head door knocker. My god that thing is beautiful, but spooky at the same time. You know I have seen their manor featured in Old West Manor Estate Magazines more than once.

So have I. Pax, do you remember when Joey received his baseball scholarship? He and his whole family were interviewed at their home, in Frank's private library. The news team from Phoenix was so impressed with the home that they later contacted the Dalecki's to see if the paper could send someone back to Bisbee to do an article regarding the manor for a Phoenix magazine that the paper owned. I think the article called it something like "Beauty Strikes in the Desert". You're right, he always seemed to have the best of everything, and anything he wanted. I remember that. They did seem to be the perfect family, and definitely the wealthiest of the community with their Import/Export Gem and Minerals business. That is no mystery though, that is a big part of what this area was built on.

Myranda I do get that; however, I still cannot shake the feeling that there is more than meets the naked eye, with their family, and possibly even their business. Wow, I act like they are dark and evil, or something. They are not, and I should be ashamed of the things I am saying to you right now. It is just that we are older, and I live here again, I just can't help but want to know more about his family. You remember how their business was always so successful even when everything else in Bisbee, and surrounding areas, were struggling with mine lay-offs. Joey always seemed to want to play that down. I think that is why I never really pushed for answers back then. There was always a bad feeling in the pit of my stomach that told me he was harboring dark secrets for his family that he could not share even with me because it could be dangerous if he did.

Dangerous, might be stretching it, but I guess he could have been hurting, and hiding something all of that time. Okay Paxy, enough about the past ghost of Joseph Dalecki. It is starting to creep me out, and besides that you are going to have your bottom lip raw if we do not change the subject. So tell me about this mystery man, as you refer to him that has you so enamored. I get the impression there is more than you are telling me.

Not really, I have never even met him actually. Our correspondence has only been via telephone.

I get that. However, you get this certain look in your eyes, start biting your bottom lip, as you always do when you are nervous, and have a completely different tone in your voice whenever you refer to him. Just like this very moment. Remind me again what it is that he does and how that involves you.

Well, he is a private investigator of sorts in the world of antiques, and arts.

Really, who was he investigating? Is it ever someone that you, or both of us know?

It is not who he investigates. It is what he investigates, fraud in antiques, and art.

So that involves you how?

Well, he hires me to consult, after he read about me, and the Brickstone in the Arizona Highways Magazine, a few months ago. You know, the article where the Brickstone was featured as one of the best Vintage Antique and Fine Art Galleries in Arizona? He said that he felt my expertise with art could be of great help to him in researching fraud pieces. I had told him that my hopes with that article were mostly that it would be beneficial to not only myself, but Bisbee as a whole. Spread the word that this quiet little community is bursting with culture, including art, theatre, music, and an energetic life style? That I have a goal to see Bisbee get more recognition for all of its present day culture, not just its past history. However, I took him up on his offer at least one time, as it would be a change from my everyday routine at the Brickstone. Also it would give me an opportunity to use my education with my degree in Fine Arts. I enjoyed our few job adventures, and it was certainly a new kind of challenge. I have no idea though, if he will ever want or need, to hire me again.

Do not try to change the subject on me by talking shop talk. I want to stay focused on what is important here. What is mystery man's name?

It is kind of sexy, Christos Artino. I like the way it rolls off of the tongue.

Paxton Steele, you are falling for this guy!

That is crazy Myranda we have never even met in person. But oh my on the telephone he sounds so delicious!

And you are biting your bottom lip Pax. Just be careful with this man with the sexy name. I don't trust him already. He may want more than your antique, and art expertise if you do hear from him again.

I doubt it. What else is there?

Pax, sometimes I just don't get you, for as smart and successful as you are you can be so naive. You are young, beautiful, single, and have a thriving business of your own. I remember in college when men were all wowed by your long out of control red curls, sapphire blue eyes, and long legs with no end on that petite body of yours. So what's not to want? Just promise me that you will not let this man seduce you over the telephone. After you meet him, of course I want to meet him, and give my approval. You know as your best friend that is definitely required.

Seduce me, that's a laugh. I am not going to even dignify that with a comment. Besides I have all I can handle in my life, or even want, with the Brickstone. I am perfectly happy alone, and have no need to complicate my life. Of course that could always change if Joey comes back.

Listen my friend, not that it is any of my business, but if it has been as long as you say it has been since you have been between the sheets with a man, I have to wonder would you even recognize the signals if he were trying. Also, if he has done his homework on you, he obviously knows that you along with the Brickstone are worth a great deal of money.

You are right it is not any of your business; however, not only are you my dearest and oldest friend along with your wonderful hubby Sam, but you are my lawyer so that makes your opinion cherished, and invaluable to me. You know that I believe that it is never a good idea to get involved with someone you are doing business with. With that being said, I think we should change the subject again, and this time away from my sexy mystery man.

Chapter Three

Back at the Brickstone I find myself wishing that mystery man would call again with another job for me. Not that I do not have plenty of other things that I should be working on, for the Brickstone. I just cannot stop thinking about him, and he is a good distraction from thinking too much about Joey. We have only worked together a few times, and everything has always started and ended on the telephone, and a check in the mail. I assume he is satisfied with our arrangement as he has never suggested a meeting face to face.

I pull out the file in my desk drawer labeled "Mystery Man". Then just as fast as I take it out I decide to put it back. I realize that there is a lot of truth to what Myranda is thinking. I have become somewhat obsessed with Christos Artino. He has this kind of sultry voice which makes it hard to even concentrate on our conversation, when he calls. There has been success with my findings in each of the small jobs that he has asked me to research for him. So hopefully he will call again. Where

I have not had much success is with my research on him. The only thing that I can find is that he has a business called, Artino Private Investigating, under Private Investigators in Newport, Virginia. I have found no reviews, or anything regarding business acquaintances, family, or wife. He is always all business when we talk, seems to be reserved, but confident.

Jilly says goodnight, and I realize that I have again buried myself in work so it is now approaching seven pm. I move to sit up straight, stretch my back, then transfer the telephone line to my apartment. Then walk over to turn out all of the lights, turn down the air-conditioning. Finally lock the front doors then go to the back corner door, of the Brickstone, that opens up to a wide all brick staircase that leads up to my apartment.

My apartment is the one place that I can always relax, be at complete peace, and block everything out that can wait, it is my private oasis. Large in comfort even though it is only twelve hundred fifty square feet. I had it restored as a living space from what was once a storage attic above the Brickstone. It opens up to a small foyer with just enough room for an antique chair, and an old refurbished flat top steamer trunk with a small tiffany lamp sitting on it. Then into the living room which has

a navy leather couch and matching love seat, and an overstuffed comfy chair which is a rose print tapestry of mauve, green, and burgundies. Then there is a lowboy chest with my television set, a coffee table and two end tables. The lowboy, and tables are antiques of Golden Oak. There is a full wall bay-window that is adorned with a beautiful tapestry floral cushion on the built in window seat under the bay window that matches the chair. The bay window overlooks onto Tombstone Canyon road. The living room separates from the efficiency kitchen by an eight by five foot black and green granite block style island that holds the sink and oven top. All full size appliances are black. On the east side of the kitchen there is a slider door that goes into a truly small bathroom and laundry room. At the other end of the apartment, which takes up half of the apartment, is my bedroom and a full bathroom that has an old refurbished six foot claw foot soaking tub. In my bedroom I have the full size iron bed that was mine growing up with the beautiful pale yellow crocheted bed throw, my grandmother Steele made for me when I graduated from College. The room is all done in creams, yellows, greens, and rose colors. Furnished with all oak antique furniture including my dresser, nightstand and an old lawyers five stack bookcase that is filled with my favorite books, and family pictures. There is another large bay window in my bedroom that is looking out towards the Mule Mountains. The large bay is roomy enough with floor space for me to use for my nightly yoga exercises. The wall behind my iron bed is done in wormy chestnut wainscoting slats. The rest of the apartment walls are all painted in a smoky greenish-gray that remind me of the beautiful Mule Mountains. Ceilings in the entire apartment are done with the same charcoal pewter sixteen inch square panels as is the Brickstone, which are reflective of the time that the building was built.

I change into my yoga clothes, put on my meditative music to begin my nightly ritual of exercise. It always helps me relax after a long day.

In the middle of my routine my land line telephone begins to ring, I leap up, and rush to answer in case it is mystery man. The voice at the other end says, hello Miss Steele this is Christos Artino I am so glad that you are still open, and able to take my call. I know that it is after seven in Arizona; however, I did not want to wait until tomorrow. I have a special request that I want to run by you, the sultry voice announces.

My heart is pounding, and I am somewhat short of breath, more from my efforts to get up quickly and run to answer the telephone before it stops ringing, than it is from my yoga exercise. Yes I reply, I am working late this evening, I lie. So what is this special request you are calling in regards to?

Actually, I am wondering if we can meet on this one. It is a bit complicated, and there is a lot to tell you before you say yes.

What date are you thinking for this meeting, Mr. Artino?

I would like to get right on this so as soon as you can get away would be great, the earlier the better.

So you want me to come to you?

Would that be a problem for you?

No, not at all. Well, I will need to check my calendar, also see if my assistant can take care of things for me while I am gone. How long are you thinking?

Not very long maybe a couple of days at the most. You will need to fly into Williamsburg Virginia. I will purchase your ticket, and book your hotel just as soon as I get the dates that you can be here.

It is not necessary for you to do those things. I can take care of it for now, and will just bill you later as part of the job, that is, if I take on the project, of course.

No arguing this is something that I will insist on if you are going to come to Virginia to consider working on this new project for me.

Okay, I will accept how you want to handle this, thank you.

Call me tomorrow morning when you have looked at your calendar, and know when you can leave.

Thank you Mr. Artino, I will.

Miss Steele please, we have done enough business together that I think it is time you call me Christos!

Okay, Christos I will contact you tomorrow morning.

I hang up the telephone almost breathless with anxiety. My god Paxton, calm yourself down. He did not say that he wants to fly you more than two thousand miles to have a red hot affair. He said he has another business project that he wants to discuss.

I immediately call Jillie to tell her that I will be out of town for a few days so she will be alone at the Brickstone. I also, need her tomorrow morning to change anything on my calendar that was scheduled for the next three days. I do not concern myself with what I might be canceling or re-scheduling. I am making meeting "mystery man" a priority. Lord only knows what has gotten into me. This type of work may be an exciting change in my everyday routine; however, it truly has nothing to do with what I normally do, and love doing. Now as my heart stops racing I realize just how exhausted I am so I treat myself to a glass of wine, and soak in a hot bath of bubbles in my claw foot tub. Then crawl into bed with my pad so that I can make some notes for Jillie.

Chapter Four

I arrive in Williamsburg, two days later in the early afternoon, and as promised there is a driver at the airport to pick me up to take me to my hotel. I am impressed with my accommodations which are more like little individual cottages that Christos booked, for my stay, while we would be discussing the project that he wanted me to consult on. Yet at the same time I am surprised it is like he has known me for years, and knows exactly what I like. It is just outside of the busy city in what I would call the rural part of Williamsburg. Quiet and peaceful, absolutely beautiful green foliage and gorgeous bright flowers in all directions that the eye can see. A natural running waterfall on the back of the property that rushes into a creek behind the cottages.

There is a note in my cottage from Christos that tells me to make myself comfortable, enjoy the quiet peaceful scenery, and just relax. He would not be available until the next day, and he would call on me for a mid-morning breakfast so as not to rush me. I think to myself, rush me? Is he kidding? He is the one that insisted that I get here as soon as possible so that we could discuss this project right away. And now he says that he does not want to rush me. What the hell does that mean? I'm not even sure why I dropped everything to come here. It's not like I need the extra work. I should be focusing on the Brickstone. Not running to Virginia to take on something that, in reality, I do not have the time to do, especially if it is as complicated as Christos made it sound. This probably means it is going to be time consuming as well. I cannot afford to ignore all of the things going on at the Brickstone. Time is money, and I need to put all of my time and energy into my business since I have only been open for only a little more than a year. I am barely breaking even financially since I bought the building, and had to renovate it before I could open the doors for business.

The next morning Christos called at eight a.m. to say that the same driver would pick me up at 9:30 sharp to drive me to where we would be having our breakfast. Odd, I wonder why he does not just come pick me up himself. Maybe he is so important that he has a full time driver, or possibly even more likely he is just too busy to take the time to drive all the way out here. However, he is the one that booked a place so far away from the city. Oh damn it I am driving myself crazy speculating about all of the unknowns regarding Christos. I cannot figure out why I am so anxious about meeting him? I feel like a school girl going on a blind date for the first time ever. I absolutely need to calm myself, remind myself, this is only a business meeting. He is probably not near as curious or nervous about meeting me. Why would he be, or even give any thought to what I look like, or anything else. He needs my expertise of vintage art once again, and nothing more. He is, I am sure much too busy to come to Bisbee so I came here. He has no idea on how my mind has fantasized all about him from the first time we spoke. Again why should he? I myself, cannot figure out this insane attraction for him that has such a magnetic pull on me. After all I have only heard his voice over the telephone, and have never seen his face even in a picture. The emotions that I feel in regards to him is so different than how I would usually be with anyone. I have worked with many artists, and done different types of business with these people in my career, and never have I felt so drawn to someone, and especially someone who has no face to me. Truly this feeling is an enigma that I do not understand. It kind of reminds me of a repeated dream that you might have where you know there has to be a hidden meaning to it, but have no idea what it is. Is there a reason that Christos has come into my life that will finally reveal itself today? I mean there has to be a reason that I am here in this place at this time meeting a mystery man that somehow has my life in such unfamiliar territory. I feel all of the control in this situation is all his.

At nine o'clock the driver is right on time. He opens my door for me, and says that we should be at our destination in about thirty minutes. I think I am going to be sick waiting another thirty minutes. I feel for some reason that this is intentional. That Christos has got me here then put off our meeting for so long, just to mess with my mind. The driver is very reserved and not at all chatty so I start the conversation by asking him if he works solely for Mr. Artino. His answer confuses me which makes me even more anxious.

His reply "no mam" I work for Mr. Artino's employer! I think to myself, his employer. Now I really am confused so say nothing back to him.

Although the drive is beautiful it seems to take forever. We park in front of a restaurant that appears to be closed. There is only one other car here that I can see so I ask, "is this where we are meeting Mr. Artino"?

Yes, Ms. Steele it is. He announces to someone from the car radio that we have, then gets out of the car to open my door.

I hesitate for a moment, before getting out. Then I ask, is this place even open?

Not this early usually. Hours are from five p.m. to midnight; however, they always make exceptions for Mr. Artino, or our employer.

My legs are shaking so bad that they can hardly hold me up, my heart is pounding, and I feel as though I am going to throw up. I tell myself if I had good sense I would run. I have no idea though, where I would run to. Also, there is the fact that I do not want to appear like I am a crazy woman even though I think maybe I have become just that.

We walk to the side door that is already open where there is a man there waiting for us dressed as a waiter in an all-black suit. He thanks the driver then states that he will show me the rest of the way to where Mr. Artino is waiting. Before the driver turns to walk away I quickly take some money from my handbag to give him. He looks at me with a kind of subtle but sly smile and says that his tip has already been taken care. Then just walks away.

Then the man in the black suit and I walk through the kitchen where there are two cooks very busily cooking, which seems odd, considering the restaurant is not even open, and there was only one car outside the Restraunt. Then in a moment we arrive to the magnificent little dining room. I immediately notice the soft music playing in the background. There are only about a dozen different size and shaped tables all topped with different vintage lace table clothes, and matching napkins. Each table has a different small chandelier hanging over it. Each one is lit, and I especially like the one where Mr. Artino is setting alone at a table for two in the center of the intimate dining room. There is just the right amount of backlighting coming from a magnificent long Mahogany bar with a beautiful beveled mirror. Off to one side of it is a young bartender standing there as if waiting for someone to request something to drink at this early hour in the day.

Even with all of this perfect ambiance surrounding me, and the mystery man that I have been fanaticizing about makes me feel again as though I may be sick to my stomach, or even faint.

He is already standing to greet me, and dismisses the waiter. He reaches for my hand then gently kisses the top of it before speaking again. The moment he speaks I feel the beats of my heart begin to slow my apprehension fading. For some reason his familiar voice has an immediate effect on me which tells me that I am in no danger with this man. He then motions for the bartender to come take our drink order. As I take in this handsome figure in front of me I would say that Christos is just shy of six feet with a strong-looking stocky build, a square-jawed face, dark green ocean eyes, and hair, plus matching beard, which is dark with the beginnings of the salt and pepper look.

Paxton, I hope you are hungry, as I am famished. I have pretty much asked for an array of breakfast specialties for the two of us. I had no idea what your pleasure would be so I just ordered everything.

Thank you I am hungry. I was told the Restraunt is not even open at this hour. Which makes me think that this is all just for you.

That is correct, breakfast here is a rarity. It is served only upon occasions such as this. This time is not just for me, but for us. I hope you will enjoy yourself as I aim to please you Ms. Steele.

Mr. Artino who are you, and what kind of occasion do you consider this to be?

Please I thought we agreed on first names.

Okay, Christos who are you?

I assure you I am only a very good business man who has made his success with private investigating of art pieces for very wealthy people, and people who desire to keep their lives and art collections private, also. You of course have already been very helpful to me with other small jobs in art forgery. You were professionally discreet as was preferred, also, very expedient in doing the jobs asked of you. Now, I find myself with a client that I could use your expertise once again. So this occasion calls that we are meeting in person for the first time so that we may discuss this particular client's needs in person, not over the telephone. As this person's privacy is of the up-most importance to them for political, or personal reasons. I hope that answers both questions to your satisfaction so that we may get on with our business, of just what it is that I need your help with this time. I hope you are okay with us discussing business as we enjoy our meal. I need us to wrap up our business this morning as I have other important matters that I must attend to later on today.

Christos, you do realize that this is really not the kind of work that I usually do, do you not?

Yes, I do realize just that, and that is another reason that you are a perfect choice for me. Now I need to tell you that I have only photos to give to you to work from of the art that we will be discussing today. The actual pieces have been stolen from my client's family. So for those political reasons that I mentioned, it is very important that we search for and find the answers that we are looking for. The art in all probability has been taken out of the country which adds much more expense and time to finding it if it comes to that. So your job of finding out whether or not the pieces are authentic, and worth finding is most important to everyone involved. If you find that they are authentic then is becomes my job to then find where the pieces are, so that hopefully, I can get them back to my client.

May I ask who the client is?

This client is an old friend of my employer's family which right now makes this a priority for me. The client is a Billionaire from Mexico who prefers to remain anonymous for many reasons; however, the most important reason to us is that we prefer that whoever stole the pieces does not get word that our client has hired someone to find the stolen art. The client had three pieces believed to be some of the original paintings by the famous Sandro Botticelli. He and his wife purchased them in Tuscany Italy several years ago at an old antique emporium that was getting ready to close their doors. Everything was priced to sell quickly, one being the Birth of Venus which was the largest of the three, the others not quite as famous, but still very much of the renaissance style. The third and smallest of the three was hanging in the master bedroom suite in a different home of our clients so it was not stolen when the other two pieces were. It still remains with the family. So we have access to it for you to examine if that would be helpful. There is of course some suspicion that the man in the antique emporium from Tuscany may have been the one that has stolen the other two pieces after all these years. He could have kept the information of where they were to be shipped after he sold them.

Christos that might especially be the case if he knew they were authentic when he sold them, and wanted to get them back one day. Maybe even to sell again as originals. I have heard of that kind of thing happening a lot in the black markets.

Yes that is true; however, that falls under my job description to investigate not yours.

Understood, I would be completely out of my scope of knowledge. Actually, I may be out of my scope and educational realm with even taking this job. Maybe I should only take on the research of who would be most qualified for you and your client, to hire, to find the information that you are needing on these art pieces.

That is not necessary, we are quite pleased with hiring you.

Our breakfast arrives. I am completely stunned looking at this beautiful array of food that is brought out for just the two of us. Are we expecting your employer, or someone other than just us to eat all of this food?

No of course not, I need this to be just us to keep it confidential.

Well Christos we cannot possibly eat all of this.

You do not know my appetite. Please though Paxton just enjoy the dishes of your liking as we discuss our business, and carefully examine some of the important things to take note of in the photos that I have to show you. Something that I should probably share with you right now is that for you to get, and be sure that the information we get, is correct, you will be traveling to Rome. You will need to visit a Monastery of Monks who have a library of books on art, and art fraud among many other topics that involve world art. This particular Monastery, is also famous for their restoration of some famous antique books of art which are housed in their reference library. These books have been restored not only because of their age, but also, because they were part of the Battle of Montecassino where one of the oldest Abbey Monasteries in Italy was bombed over seventy five years ago. A big part of what the Monastery library is used for today is to research the authenticity of rare art. This particular Monastery is also, known for their individual brilliant knowledges of authenticity of art pieces and most importantly forgery. The Monk that you will need to ask for, then speak with in this matter, is an older Monk named Nick. I have been told he is the best in the world for his knowledge of art.

Christos, again, who are you, and who is your employer?

He faces me straight on with a look in his eyes that would terrify anyone.

In a deep sharp voice he says: Paxton, I am a Professional Private Investigator who investigates fraud in high end collectables and art. I work for important people whose identity is not relevant to what I need from you. There really is very little I can, or will share of my work cases as they are mostly of confidential matters. So please stop with the questions that are not relevant to why we are meeting today.

Okay, Christos then just one last thing. Why on earth do you want my help? You must know that, other than Art School, I am self-taught about rare art pieces. I own and operate a small gallery in Southern Arizona that most everyone in the big picture of the art world has never even heard of, or ever will.

Hiring you is a benefit, as you and your Gallery, as you just said yourself, are for the most part low profile. I do not mean to sound disrespectable, but you are asking for the truth so here it is. This type of work sometimes takes someone that would never be suspected of looking into the most valuable art pieces worth many millions of dollars. We need someone that can do this under the radar so we came to you.

Mr. Artino, I am pretty sure that this is not a compliment, also it is nice to know that the only thing that I mean to you, and your employer who ever the hell that may be, is that I am so insignificant in the real world of art that you feel that it is safe for me to be bought, and to be used to your benefit. I will be sure to add this to my resume if I am ever looking to do work such as this any other time.

Paxton simmer down that is not what I said, and certainly did not mean to imply that by any means. There was a great deal of research done to find the perfect, highly intelligent, art savvy person that you are, before I called you. Or ever offered my business to you, and remember no one forced you to say yes to my offers.

Well so much for your story of finding me in the Arizona Highway Magazine.

You are wrong Paxton that is exactly where my employer first read about you, along with your new business the Brickstone Antique & Art Gallery. Also, the Brickstone was highly recommended by someone that he is acquainted professionally with. I am afraid that I cannot remember their names only that they had been in your Gallery on a road trip through Arizona. Then of course you were checked out to see if you would be a legitimate qualified art person to work for us. Before you ask the answer to your next question is yes, the other small jobs that we asked you to do were more or less opportunities for us to see if you could handle the bigger ones like this. That is the reason we are finally taking the time to meet in person, and asking you to take on something much bigger with more importance attached to it.

Okay, I have no idea why, but I guess I can accept that. It makes me feel somewhat better that you feel that I am so capable. However, now for my peace of mind question, and please be honest. Is what you do, or any of what I am going to be asked to do, illegal?

Not hardly Paxton I am a legitimate Professional as I have already explained to you. My work is to find the guilty. I have to sometimes hire someone to work for me that will not be suspected as any kind of law officer, or PI. Also, people do not usually hire someone like me if there case does not need to be kept private. They could just go to the police if privacy or priority, to them, were not of any importance.

Now at this moment I am still wondering what I am getting myself into. Especially when I hear myself say let's get to it then.

Paxton, I am pleased to hear you say this. For a few minutes there I thought you were going to say no, and get up and run.

I started laughing, and shared with him that, I did think about running away this morning before we even had this conversation, but I did not know exactly where I was, or where I would run to.

We then discussed the rest of the details of what was expected before I signed the confidentiality contract that he placed in front of me. All my expenses would be paid even if I needed to make several trips back to Rome. That was that, Christos called his driver to pick me up to take me back to the cottage. Before I left he made it clear that we would need to always be in close contact regarding my findings. He asked me to call him after I returned to Arizona, and had time to make the plans that I needed to make ,at the Brickstone, so that I would be able to leave for Rome, and concentrate on nothing other than my knew task at hand. He said he would then take care of everything else that had to be done. I certainly had no doubt that he would do exactly that.

Forty minutes later I am back at the cottage all alone thinking about how all of this might change my entire life, especially the dollar amount of what I was going to be paid for this job. Also, something that now could not be any clearer to me was that Christos Artino had no romantic intentions towards me. Since I was booked for one more night I decided that I wanted some wine, lots of wine.

Chapter Five

How am I going to explain this to anyone, especially Jillie Townsend my assistant at the Brickstone, and my best friend from grade school, Myranda? Taking this job could take weeks, or even months. That means that I will have to talk to Jillie about her taking more responsibility at the Brickstone. Myranda, of course, is going to ask me how this new plan makes good business sense or fits into my plan to make the Brickstone the best and most famous Antique and Art Gallery in Arizona. I have no idea how to answer that question other than the money that I will be paid is significant enough to help tremendously with the ideas and dreams that I have for the Brickstone. Yet I keep asking myself, what makes this man so intriguing to me where in so many ways he is still a complete stranger? Maybe the mystery of it all is what has me intrigued, and completely hooked on this adventure. My whole life I seem to be ready for the next adventure whatever it might be.

Six days later, with my passport in hand, all of the plans are in place, and I am on a jet to the Leonardo da Vinci- Fiumicino Airport in Rome, Italy.

Now in Rome my hotel is the exquisite Boscolo Exedra, a 19th Century Palace. I keep asking myself how it is that Christos always seems to know where to make reservations that would be to my exact taste. I know it has to be just a crazy coincidence because we have never spoken to each other in a personal way so that he could possibly know me well enough to know my tastes, or maybe it is just that we both have the same impeccably good taste.

I have, of course, done my homework before I get here and know that there are only certain times of day that the Monastery is open to visitors. That means that I have some time to do some touring around the city. Maybe find a sidewalk café or Bistro for lunch. The hotel is right in the center of Historic Rome in walking distance to many places such as the Colosseum, Vatican, Roman Forum, Spanish Steps, and the Pantheon. I want to see them all before I go back to the United States. I was also advised, when doing my research, that if I was fortunate enough to be staying in the historic center part of Rome the best way to go from place to place would certainly be to walk. Transportation is limited, also it is easier this way to appreciate the many smaller venues that I might otherwise most likely miss if sightseeing by bus, or car. Everything would be just as accessible by foot.

I find myself biting my bottom lip as I have had this strange feeling that someone was following me from the very moment that I left the Boscolo Exedra Palace. That is impossible I tell myself. I do not even know anyone in Rome. I am just being paranoid due to all of the secrecy and confidentiality of my mission on this visit. So I try to calm myself, and only concentrate on the most magnificent sights of this old, and glamorous city, plus enjoy my sandwich and soup that I have just ordered.

Later that day at 7:00 p.m., after the dinner hour at the Monastery, I arrive and have a very successful visit with the Bishop Nick, who is no longer a Monk, but is now much higher in the hierarchy of the Roman Catholic Church. He is very much interested in helping me find the answers to the art pieces in question. We both agree that it will be more difficult, having only pictures of the two that were taken, but having the small painting with me for him to examine is a big help. He is optimistic that it is almost certain that the three paintings were done by the same artist.

Bishop Nick asks that I meet him the next morning at the Monastery for early Mass at 5:00 a.m. Then for breakfast, to discuss further the expectation and timeframe for the task of finding out the authenticity of the paintings.

When I return to the Palace I cannot help but think of Bishop Nick's enthusiasm regarding our work together, also what a kind and gentle man he seems to be. I am now for the first time truly excited that I said yes to Christos. I now have such optimism that this experience is going to be much more than just a job that I agreed to do, but maybe very monumental, and possibly life changing for me. I am excited to be able to take back to Bisbee the knowledge about rare art that I can soak up from spending time at the Monastery with the Monks, and of course Bishop Nick. It is now 10:00 pm in Italy which makes it 2:00 p.m. in Arizona, so I call Jillie to see how things are at the Brickstone. I have asked a lot of her, in my absence, besides continuing to update all of our inventory in the new program software that I just purchased for the Brickstone. Then I call to talk to Myranda. All this time keeping in mind that even though my cell phone works pretty well from Italy it is very expensive. Of course Christos is paying this bill, also.

Myranda, I am so excited about being here. It is a beautiful country and the city of Rome is amazing, and so beautiful. The Italian people are so friendly even though my Italian is not very good. They are all so willing to help me in any way that they can. Most everyone that I have tried to communicate with speaks some English, or at least can understand what I am trying to tell them, by some miracle. There are a few English speaking people here at the hotel, or should I say at the Boscolo Exedra Palace, which is so helpful. I love pronouncing the name of this hotel. It sounds as exquisite as it truly is. Elegant and beautiful, it is actually an old renovated Palace that is from the 19th Century. I will take lots of pictures to show you when I return home.

Pax, do you think that you are going to be able to accomplish what you went to Rome for?

Definitely, I have already been to the Monastery, and met with the Bishop who is going to be the point man along with other Monks that will be working on this for me. I have been invited back tomorrow morning for Mass and breakfast. I suppose we will finish up what we need to discuss for them to start on this project. I am going to get a tour of the entire Monastery, including their art library. I will probably spend most of my days that I have left here, reading their books and picking their brains for everything that I can learn. Then it seems my work here will be done, until I hear back from them. Hopefully they will have the information we need. It all now seems so easy. I have no idea why I was so worried.

Worried, you did not share with me that you were worried.

Well of course I was a little worried just knowing that this is an enormous task for me to take on since I do not have this type of experience. Oh Myranda, I wish you could be here with me. This place is all so incredible, you have to see it to understand what I am talking about. I can't believe that I never wanted to come here before now. Of course it would all be more beautiful and romantic to be here with a man that you love. You and Sam must plan your next trip to be Italy. I promise you will not be disappointed. Well I guess I better say goodnight as it is already late here, and I need to be at the Monastery for a 5:00 a.m. Mass, and then breakfast. I just wanted to check in so that you would not worry. I probably will not call, maybe once more, it is so expensive, and I do not want Christos to think that I was too extravagant on my first trip to Italy. It still feels a little like a dream to me that I am here doing what I am doing.

Are you kidding me did you say Mass at 5:00 a.m. That is not something that I see, the Paxton I know doing, even though you are Catholic?

I know, and I did not even blink when Bishop Nick told me how early I needed to be there tomorrow. It must be the air, but I can hardly wait. I will stay in touch. Talk to you soon, luv ya!

Chapter Six

A few weeks later back in Bisbee, after what I would consider a successful working trip to Rome, I open the doors to the Brickstone just in time to hear the telephone ringing. I have my arms full so I decide to let the answering machine get the message. I also, still have everything circling in my mind of all the many things that I need to accomplish today. I am going to Tucson tomorrow morning to fly out for a buying trip in Colorado. To the World Wide Antiques and Art Show, in Denver. Hopefully to find, and purchase several original, rare, one of a kind prints, and art masterpieces. Business has been good so my merchandise is as low as it has been in a long time.

I want to look for some pieces by Vincent William van Gogh whose style is mostly Western art. Several of my customers that are from the four corners area of Arizona, Utah, Colorado, and New Mexico are most interested in this style. Also, I am running low in these types of beautiful art work. I usually look for artworks that include oil paintings as well as impressionist pieces. Obviously, I would love to purchase a van Gogh; however, financially the time to do that has not arrived. I do try to look though for pieces that have his style of brushwork, bold colors, and dramatic sense of humor.

I will be gone four days so the first thing that I need to do is make sure that my assistant Jillie Townsend and I meet to go over everything that needs to be taken care of while I am absent from the Brickstone. She is a sweetheart, and I count on her in my life almost as much as I do Myranda. She is a graduate of the School of Art Institute in Chicago. Little did I know that when I advertised for a personal assistant in most of the country's best art schools that I would find someone so energetic, driven, and so business savvy also, with a minor in business. I interviewed her twice, once on the telephone, then I had her come to Bisbee for her second interview. Jillie is a pretty young woman with a five foot three inch build, long straight nutmeg brown hair that falls below her shoulders, and the deepest brown eyes. I wanted her to experience in person the charm and aura of our little community in southern Arizona, it cannot be explained. I have heard many people say that Bisbee is one of the "best little kept secrets," in all of America. Others never quite understand the cherished aura of the seventies that seemed to embrace Bisbee, and held on tight. The seventies also, gave our town a love of art, music, and a mostly quiet lifestyle compared to the lifestyle of a city. Jillie though, fell in love with Bisbee, and the Brickstone immediately. She has the charm of a small town girl, the knowledge of a veteran art dealer, and never comes across as pushy. This is why everyone that comes through the doors of the Brickstone immediately fall in love with her. Her sense of humor and smile are contagious. She has a passion for life, and for her work.

Once in Denver, I get checked into my hotel that is on the same property as the show. Then I immediately go check in as a buyer at the show. I see several vendors that I have become friends with over the years, even before I came as a business owner. I first started coming to this wonderful show to make purchases for myself. There are three shows a year, one in the spring, summer, and fall. I try to make all three. They are at the Denver Mart Expo Center. There is always around 500 antique and vintage dealers from around the United States, plus a few other countries. Each of the dealers travels the globe to bring new and unique pieces to the shows. Everything from art, furniture and collectables that the mind can imagine.

I spent this first day looking at everything, as I always do. So now I will go back to my hotel room, order some dinner from room service, and then start going over my list and description of some of the things that I am interested in, possibly purchasing, if I can make the deals, for the right prices.

I usually will only look at things that can be mailed back to the Brickstone. So very rarely do I purchase antique furniture. I am more interested in first edition books, small collectibles, Victorian tiffany lamps, and beautiful signed art pieces from all over the world. I try to purchase my furniture from closer destinations that I can easily have picked up, or delivered.

The telephone in my hotel room rings just as I am finishing my dinner. It is Jillie, she is so excited that I can hardly understand what she is saying. Jillie, calm down take a deep breath I cannot make out what you are telling me.

Pax, you will not believe what I am going to tell you.

You met the love of your life, you are getting married this weekend and want to know if I will be your maid of honor? There is this long pause from Jillie. Then finally she speaks again still in a very exuberant voice.

No, but there is a gentleman that left two voice mails yesterday, before I was able to get back with him. He first asked to speak directly to you. I told him you were out of state on a buying trip. You had probably not even left on your flight when he left the first message. Anyway, he will be arriving at the Brickstone early next week from Annapolis Maryland to purchase as many as twenty five of our most expensive landscape art pieces. Also, he is interested in some of our portrait pieces that I told him about. I made an inventory list of some things that he may be interested in, when he arrives. If he purchases as much as he says he is going to, this could be just what we need to have the capital to do the things at the Brickstone that we have been dreaming about doing.

Well did he give a name, or a business that he is associated with? This could be some kind of scam you know.

He gave me the name Mr. Travis Gary. He sounded like he knew what he was talking about regarding art. Also, very sure of what he wanted. He had apparently done his homework as he seemed to be sure that we would have exactly what he was looking for. He asked what day exactly you would be returning. He wants to make the trip here, when you return, to look at the suggested pieces, and to meet you in person. He would like for us to have already picked out our finest pieces to show him when he arrives, as not to waste any time. Also, he inquired about where would be the most trusted place to wrap them securely for shipping. I told him that you and I would discuss that, but I told him my first suggestion would probably be the Bisbee post office right down the street. He said if it is agreeable to you he will have the money directly wired to our business account before having the pieces sent to him.

That's it Jillie, he didn't say anything else like what his purchases were for?

No actually he didn't, but, can you believe what I am telling you?

No, actually I can't, but l hope that it is all truly on the up and up. If this is for real I better purchase double what I thought that I was going to be purchasing. If he calls again make sure to get all of the specifics that he will give you. I would like to buy some pieces that may be specific to his taste. I have two more full days to shop so that gives me plenty of time. Jillie make sure to get all the information that you can, such as if he needs us to arrange transportation or hotel accommodations for him while he is in Bisbee. If he does, you know how I feel about the Copper Queen, call them and arrange for their best suite, please. I would like to see where he is flying into and make all arrangements to have him picked up at the airport. Hope he realizes that we do not have an airport in Bisbee. If he is arriving early next week I guess there is no reason to ask for a notarized letter of good faith. But, I will call Myranda to ask how to handle the money transfer before we agree to anything.

Myranda agreed with my opinion that it is quite common for large quantities of art to be purchased in a single buying trip at large galleries. It would also, make since that it would behoove a buyer to look around at smaller galleries for better prices. Another thing that is quite common for some interior decorators to do is to go to galleries and purchase everything they need all at once for a particular home or corporation.

We are both curious though to how or why someone, that is making a purchase of this nature from Maryland, would come all the way to a small town in Arizona for the art pieces. Her advice to me is to just make sure that I contact my bank when the money is transferred to make sure that everything is final before I release his purchases. And, that our banks talk directly to each other so there are no account numbers exchanged between him and me. She said it is always better to be just a fraction sceptic, and safe so as not to be taken advantage of, there are a lot of scam creeps out there. I agree with her on this completely, after all that is what Christos's work is all about.

Then after talking to her, the next two days I work like a

shopping-maniac. Like I was spending someone else's money, I may add. Mostly shopping for American Art, as that seems to be what is most popular today. Modern and contemporary art that represents themes and trends not otherwise available in most small galleries due to the nature of the high expense. I always like to look for pieces that have a range of broad diversity in artistic practices in America. Pieces by some of the most provocative artists that have given America expressive art, figurative art, dramatic art, and of course my favorite is the historic vernacular art of war times. I was also, able to pick up some of my favorite rare framed works of the crusading legal cartoon prints from the late eighteen hundreds by the artist Thomas Nast who once was noted as one of the most influential artists, next to Walt Disney, due to his children characters, and his depiction of the iconic drawings of Santa Claus. Nast was considered to be the "Father of the American Cartoon." His drawing were made famous in the Harper's Weekly and the New York Times. He popularized the donkey to the Democratic Party and the elephant to the Republican Party was said to have reelected Lincoln in 1864. Also, Grant in 1886 said that he contributed his election partly due to the pencil of Nast. In the summer of 1862 Nast had a position with the Harper's Weekly. He would visit battlefields to send reportorial sketches back to the magazine. His drawings were transformed by engravers into wood engravings that were often printed as double spreads about twenty inches wide. Nast was skillful at using allegory and melodrama in his art. Other than the art pieces the only other things that I purchase are two very ornate Old World Victorian lamps, and twelve very unique antique mirrors from Pennsylvania of all different shapes and sizes, with Gingerbread type frames.

Chapter Seven

When I return Jillie and Mr. Travis Gary have already set up our appointment. Mr. Gary declined my offer to have a driver waiting for him at the airport. I have asked a local art appraiser that we have worked with in the past, Mr. Casey Brandt to be present.

I have to admit that I was nervous of the upcoming meeting. Never have I had such a potentially large sale at the Brickstone in one day, to one buyer. My sales usually are to a local patron, or a tourist who purchases one or two pieces. I wanted to make sure that Jillie and I had every piece that he may be interested in, staged perfectly. Plus there were the pieces to add into the mix that I had shipped with two day shipping from the show in Denver.

Our meeting went exceptionally well with a profit of twenty seven thousand being wired to my business account with absolutely no hiccups. I found Mr. Gary to be quite pleasant to work with. He seemed to be very knowledgeable, well educated in art, also, he knew something of the artist and history of every piece that he purchased from us. After completing our business acquisitions Mr. Brandt left, and Jillie was busy helping other customers. Mr. Gary and I continued to have a nice conversation regarding the history of Bisbee, also what made me come back to Bisbee to open the Brickstone. I enjoyed our conversation quite immensely. Before he left for his drive back to Tucson, for his early morning flight the next day, we left our conversation with the satisfaction that we both looked forward to doing business together again one day. Wow, I was exhausted. That evening when I went up to my apartment. Myranda had called and asked me to join her and Sam for dinner. She wanted to hear all about Mr. Gary and what pieces he had taken; however, I just wanted to do my Yoga, shower, and collapse into my bed. I sometimes think that it is days and nights like this that may be the reason that I am still single. My social life until just recently, with the projects that I have taken on for Christos, are pretty much just days at the Brickstone. With a few buying trips here and there where I have gotten to be friends with some of the other buyers, and a few of my favorite venders. Funny thing is though, I am happy with exactly how my life is. I went to school, I traveled, and I worked hard at a couple of other Art Galleries in Colorado, saved my money. With that and my inheritance from my parents I was able to come back to Bisbee to open up my own dream Antique and Art Gallery. What more do I need? Unless of course Joey ever comes back to Bisbee.

The next day started with quite the surprise, and puzzle. Jillie brings to my attention that she found a pocket size business card folder on the floor under the drawing table in our show room where we had displayed each piece of art under lighting, for Mr. Gary to examine, along with the art appraiser Casey Brandt. She said that there were only three business cards in it. One belonging to a gentleman named Craig Thomas, who was the owner of the Thomas Funeral Home and Crematorium in Annapolis Maryland, a Ms. Johnna Hannah, a Real Estate Attorney in Annapolis Maryland, and a Mr. Christos Artino (Independent Private Investigator) from Newport Virginia. But hand written on back of his business card was the name Mr. Joseph Dalecki (Special Agent) for Narcotics and Special Investigations Division (NSID) Metropolitan Police Department- Washington, DC. 20001 circled in red ink. Now it is possible that Casey Brandt would maybe know Joseph Dalecki; however, very unlikely that he would have other business cards from Annapolis Maryland, where Mr. Gary was from. This of course means that the business card folder belonged to Mr. Travis Gary. Now I am immediately furious, not to mention more than a little suspicious, of the gentleman that I had just the day before liked so much, and thought so highly of.

I of course call Myranda to see what she thinks I should do.

Pax this whole thing screams foul. Obviously there is something wrong, we both know it. I think we have both known from the first time Travis Gary called Jillie, to set up an appointment. We both so badly wanted to believe that it was just good fortune that he had heard of the Brickstone, in quaint little Bisbee, and wanted to make you rich in one day, ha-ha. These type of sales rarely happen except in large cities, and in world renowned galleries. Dammit, I should have done some checking for you when you called me from Denver. At that time, even though it may have sounded sketchy, we were not even sure he would show up. Then it all happened so fast. Okay, well too late for that; however, now I want you to check your bank account to make sure the money has not been reversed. Then if it is still in your account move all of it to another account possibly your personal account, just for now. No I have a better idea, I am going to set up a short term account for my law practice. You check your bank account first. Call me back in thirty minutes. I will have an account number for you to deposit the money in to. I do not want you to transfer it by bank wire, so withdraw it, then you will hand deposit it at my bank in the new account. I won't be available again until after six this evening. I have just enough time if I leave now to go to upper Bisbee to the Bank so I can get that account set up, and give you the number. I have a court case today that will have me unavailable for the rest of the day. After you have moved the money your next step is to call him, be very direct with him, tell him that you found his business card folder, and want to know how he is connected to Christos Artino. Also, changing the subject for a moment, did you hear about the murder last night in our quiet little town?

Myranda, are you kidding me? Murder in Bisbee. This is not the early 1900's. Who on earth was murdered?

Laura Pilner.

No, who in hell would murder Laura?

I mostly have street gossip about it right now. So I called my friend Detective Zen Marlowe who collaborated the story. He said they had very little to go on at this time. What they did have he could not discuss with me.

Where did it happen?

It happened somewhere on OK Street late last night. Apparently she had just left the Mayors home where she had attended a small dinner party. Everyone that attended is being questioned today, of course. The party was apparently in part to discuss next year's Great Stair Climb.

After we hang up I immediately tell Jillie that I need to make a trip to the bank. The money was still in my account so I did as Myranda suggested. Moved the money from one account to the other. I then called Mr. Gary, and told him that I had found his business card folder on my floor of the gallery, so I would like for him to explain his connection to Christos Artino. This news did not really seem to get much of a reaction from him. He just replies that it is unfortunate that he left his folder; however, I would need to speak with Mr. Artino, myself, for any information regarding their acquaintance. He tells me that he will call Mr. Artino to ask him to call me to discuss this. Then he thanks me again for having the art pieces sent to his address in Maryland, says that it was a pleasure to meet me, and then immediately hangs up. I feel a shiver go all the way up my spine, I feel myself biting my bottom lip, raw. Something is just so wrong, this was definitely no coincidence. At Myranda's office the next day she tells me that the reason she wanted the money in a different account, totally separate from my accounts, is that maybe the money is stolen funds. If that is the case she does not want Travis Gary to have the ability to have the money reversed if something illegal is going on, and he knows we are on to him. Now I am actually shaking and wondering if I have put myself, along with the Brickstone, in the middle of something illegal.

Pax I also plan on contacting Mr. Christos Artino myself today as your attorney via a letter. I want him to be aware that you have hired me to represent you as your personal attorney.

I will send this letter certified requesting his signature. It will read something to the effect of, as your attorney I have been appointed to notify him that you will no longer be working on the case of the stolen art for his anonymous client, or be accepting any work cases offered by him,, until which time he is able to explain, to your satisfaction, his connection to one Mr. Travis Gary. This information is to be given only in written form on his letterhead paper signed by himself within the next two weeks. He is not to try and contact you by telephone, or in any other way. If a written letter is not received within two weeks' time he will be deleted from the professional list of Ms. Paxton Steele, and will be asked not to contact or harass you in any form of communication. If he does so legal action may be taken against him in the form of a harassment restraining order.

Myranda doesn't this all seem just a little extreme? Do you think this is truly necessary at this time?

Paxton, do you want to risk yourself along with your reputation, or the Brickstone to being involved with something of questionable nature? I have always had a somewhat uneasy feeling about your Mr. Christos Artino too, and now you make a twenty eight thousand dollar acquisition with another "mystery man" Travis Gary, that comes all the way from Maryland to purchase art from a small gallery in a small Arizona town. Tells you he cannot remember exactly how his employer heard about the Brickstone other than a one-time only article that was in the Arizona Highways Magazine, but he remembers it was recommended very favorably, by an un-named art enthusiast that dropped in on a road trip though Arizona. Then quite by accident you find that Mr. Gary has, un-known to you, connections of some kind to Mr. Artino. Then lastly but possibly not the most insignificant is, he has Joey's information hand written on the back of Artino's card. No, I do not think that our actions are too extreme! These are the kinds of things that you pay me for as your attorney. Let me do what I think is needed, and best for you, please. We will wait to see what his response will be, then we can respond accordingly. A person's reaction to any situation usually tells you everything you need to know.

Chapter Eight

I keep myself busy at Brickstone the next couple of weeks. Jillie usually does most of our staging, weekly, to fill the voids of things that have been purchased, or just changing everything around so that there is always a fresh look in the Gallery. I forgot how much I like to do these things too, so I am putting myself in the thick of everything right now so that I do not have time to let my mind wonder to dark places. After arranging some fresh flowers I decide to completely rearrange all of the furniture in the entire gallery. Then I move on to staging the silver, ceramic and porcelain dolls, the beautiful old clocks, along with the exquisite paintings that I just purchased. I cannot stop thinking though of the fact that we have not heard a word from Christos which has me somewhat puzzled, and a whole lot angry. I lately find myself, not much in the mood to do anything other than work, today was no different. It is getting late so I go upstairs to my usual routine of un-winding, to Yoga, a hot bath with some red wine. Then I find myself in bed alone looking at one of the magazines, or catalogs that I have stacks of on the newest gallery designs. Some life for a single twenty eight year old woman that I have carved out for myself.

The next morning Jillie says to me, maybe it would be a good idea for you to start the ball rolling on a new project by calling Charlotte Dalecki to see if she is still interested in looking at new art for the manor.

You know Jillie that is a fantastic idea, and maybe I can get her to share something with me regarding Joey. Here almost right out of the blue sky his contact information just falls into my lap, or should I say onto the floor of the Brickstone. That has to mean something, but I am not sure that I have the nerve to find out what that something is. I can't explain my feelings, or why I cannot bring myself to call him to ask if maybe he could clear any of this up for me. After all I have a phone number for him now. But for today though I will just settle on calling his mother, and see if that might lead somewhere. Years ago she and I did have a kind of relationship, of sorts. I will start the conversation by sharing with her that I have recently purchased some exquisite new pieces at a buying market in Denver. Pieces that bring the beautiful manor into mind. Yes, that is exactly what I will do, then I should be able to find a way to bring up the strange coincidence that occurred here with the business cards. Then possibly when she visits with Joey again she will bring it up, even if she is unwilling to talk about him with me. That might at least give him the idea or an excuse to call me. Jillie, I cannot imagine what I would ever do without you, you are genius!

The next day is Sunday morning, and so that means I am on the veranda at the Copper Queen having my cinnamon tea with toast making a list of things that I want to share with Charlotte tomorrow, when we meet. She seemed very excited to see what I had in mind for the manor. Then at that very moment someone walks up behind me puts their hands over my eyes and says in a low voice, do I detect that you still have that habit of biting your bottom lip when you are in deep thought, or maybe nervous. I just freeze, it cannot possibly be who it sounds like.

Paxton Steele I would feel better if you would turn around to give me a long, long, overdue hug, maybe even a long overdue kiss.

I turn around jump up to put my arms around the best looking man I have ever known, Joey Dalecki. For a moment I am lost in the only cologne that I have ever known him to wear, "Aramis." Somehow between the cologne and that deep voice, I feel paralyzed, I cannot speak, nor do I want to move out of his arms. If this is a dream, please God do not ever let me wake up! Just let this man keep kissing me.

Paxy, you have not changed, nor has your kiss.

He pushes me back to stare as if drinking my whole body in with those deep brown eyes. He is already telling me that he has had an unexplainable craving for me from the first time he saw me years earlier at a little league ball game. Nothing has ever changed between us. Absence has only had the effect of making those feelings stronger. What has taken us so long, Ms. Paxton Steele?

I catch my breath, what are you doing in Bisbee?

I came in yesterday went straight to the manor to see my parents, but I could not make myself come see you, when I first arrived, because I still needed some time to collect my thoughts. Trying to decide how to say the things I wanted, hell, needed to say to you. I cannot make the same mistakes that I made ten years ago wondering how to tell you, or if I should tell you, and risk our friendship. Paxton Steele I love you, and I hope you love me.

I am thinking to myself, I have always been enamored with him from the very beginning of our friendship. I can feel my heart

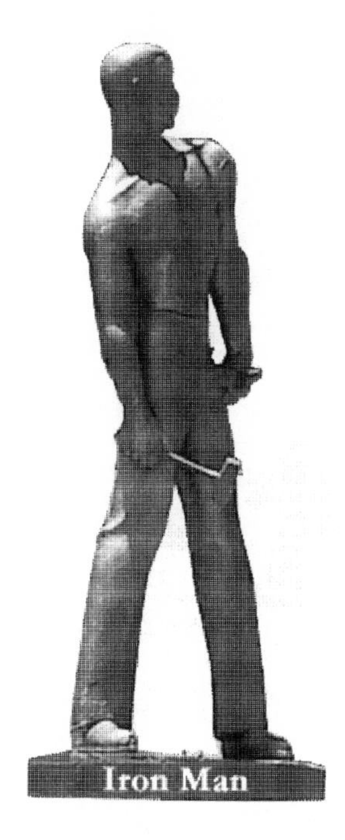

pounding hard in my chest, my breath seems to leave me again, and my head is spinning. Joey is even better looking now as a grown man, with his deep dark black hair, his gorgeous skin tone, the color of hot chocolate, He still has that kind of Don Johnson Miami Vice look, those pooling brown eyes, he is about 6'2" tall, but now with a body more like the Ironman Statue that stands with such integrity at the bottom of Quality Hill by the courthouse. LOL ..... maybe not quite! I catch my breath once again, and find my voice, I have always loved you, Joey Dalecki!

Chapter Nine

Monday his mother forgives me for cancelling our appointment so that I can spend the day with her son. Jillie will be fine at the Brickstone, alone today. Joey and I have made plans to spend the entire day catching up, in my apartment. We spent almost the entire day talking about the loss of my parents, and the Brickstone, my dream. We finally take time to make finger sandwiches to eat, along with some fruit with whipped topping for what is now an early dinner. It was definitely time to get something in our stomachs. We had finished two bottles of wine in the lost time of our conversation. Afterward he stands next to me, at the sink, to dry the few dishes after I have washed them. With this small task taken care of he decides to mush me up against the kitchen wall. He is kissing me, his hands are rubbing me up and down my body. A sensation that is sending a warm pooling liquid low in my belly, and even lower. I can feel his raw sexual power as he is grinding his body up against mine. I let out a soft moan, and run my fingers through his hair. Then suddenly, I know that I can go no farther. I pull back taking my mouth from his to say stop. I do not want this to turn into a fiery seduction, and that is what this teasing make out session will turn in too. He then, with a tight grip on both shoulders, stares deep into my eyes with his dark brown eyes, and with a very seductive throaty voice says to me, who is teasing. Then picks me up in one quick swoop, my hair dangling from one end, and my bare feet from the other end. In his arms he then carries me out of the kitchen, and to my bedroom. Then onto the bed, and crawls so easily on top of me with the force of all his weight so that I cannot begin to resist.

Paxy, I'm in love with you! I want you right now. I have waited for this very moment, of you and me, for way too long.

Even hearing his words I resist, by pushing hard up against his chest, holding back my frustrated passion, and whisper in a low quiet voice, Joey please slow down I am not sure we are ready for this to happen. He pulls himself up very quickly looks in to my eyes one again, and with such an honest hurt look in his eyes says, damn-it Paxy, your timing, to say stop, sucks. He does stop, then completely lifts himself off of me, gets off the bed, and walks out of the bedroom cussing to himself. I am pretty sure he is cussing in Italian, from what I can understand, which is very little. I get the feeling that he is not used to having someone say no. I follow him into my living room. Joey, I am sorry, but yesterday was the first time we have seen each other in over ten years. We need to talk first, and probably with our clothes on would be a good idea.

I doubt that clothes will make our conversation more interesting Paxy, actually I think quite the opposite. I do agree there is much we have to talk about, but it might be more fun naked.

I start laughing as does he. Seriously though Joey you may have all of your thoughts together, but mine are still very scattered. I am not even sure where to begin. There are so many things that we should talk about. Plus there are some questions that I want to ask you about something that just happened, involving the Brickstone. Where our conversation needs to begin is kind of overwhelming to me.

Baby Doll we have two weeks to talk about everything that needs to be talked about, before, I will need to leave back to Washington, to tie up some loose ends. Then I am going to take a leave of absence from the agency so that I can spend some time with you, and my family. But right now all I want is to spend, what is left of this day, and the entire night, with you. I want this more than anything else in this world. I am pretty sure that anything we have to clear the air about, or any answers that you may want from me, can wait for another few hours. You are right, it has been ten years since we have seen each other.

I have not been called "Baby Doll" in the last ten years, and you did not tell me yesterday why you are taking a leave of absence.

I hope you have not, I like to think that name is reserved for only me to call you! And I will explain my leave of absence soon enough.

I move very close to him, so close that I can slide my arms around his neck, then with the weight of my entire body make him fall back onto the couch. This time though I am on top which gives me some control of how this will probably go. The heat is washing over both of us as our bodies start pushing into each other, with a slow, but powerful need. Our lips are parted just enough on each other's mouths so that we can taste the desire we both have for each other. He puts a hand under my top so that he can feel my breast, he is now kissing me softly, and sliding his lips down my neck exploring me before he gets to my hard nipple. He then suckles one breast, then the other, with so much fever and passion that I have a mini climax. He seems to sense just how sensitive my breasts are. He is now tracing them one at a time with his fingertips. Then before I know what is happening he has my jeans pushed down, and off. We are aching for each other. We have now made our way to the floor onto the large hand woven antique throw rug. In the next moment with what seems like we have both been waiting for our entire lives he is undressed, and on top of me, and with one hard thrust he is inside me. Now moving as if we are woven together as one, we spend the next hour with our bodies entwined in complete explosions of one climax after another.

I wake up still on the soft rug; however, Joey, sometime in the night, must have searched out for the quilt, that I am now underneath. I realize it is only five thirty in the morning, and I find this naked man, with his lean muscular body, just staring out the bay window, in my living room, at the pouring rain, also looking like he is a million miles away in deep thought. I immediately remember our wonderful night together with our bodies, flesh on flesh, that were so hungry for each other. I get up quietly, put on nothing more than the pullover silk top that is laying on the floor. I walk over to him, slide my arms around his waist, just to hold him tight. For some reason I just know, without any explanation that we are both thinking of the conversation ahead of us that might change everything. It is like some type of loss has already happened before we even say good morning, even though last night felt as if we had come full circle back to each other.

He turns around so that we are facing each other, but staying in each other's arms, then speaks Paxy, I want you to know that last night was the most meaningful time that I have ever spent with any woman, and I knew it would be. I would like to think that I saved the very best for last so that I could spend the rest of my life with you.

But.

We need to talk about why I am here, and how that may affect us.

Joey, I think what you are trying to tell me is that the reason you are here has something to do with the two men that have mysteriously come into my life lately. Because you could definitely say that my life has been affected by my meeting both of them. Then my life is once again affected by your reappearance. I know for a fact that the three of you are all acquainted. So I am more than just a little interested in your explanation of how it all ties together.

You are right Paxy, and you have every right to be curious of the details. I need some coffee though before we begin this conversation. I also, want to shower, then let me fix you breakfast. We will eat then go for a drive. I for some reason feel that it will be easier to share everything with you if we are driving somewhere, or anywhere away from Bisbee. If we stay here in your apartment all day, again, I will not be in any mood to talk about all of this. I am only going to want take you to bed, over and over again.

Chapter Ten

After a quick breakfast that neither one of us really ate much of due to thinking of the pending drive, and conversation ahead of us, we headed north going towards Tombstone. First thing that popped into my mind was how much Joey and I used to love spending time there when we were younger. As a matter of fact we drove there for my sixteenth birthday, went to the famous Crystal Palace, had pizza with vanilla cokes, and then we danced. I still have the large mug from there that he bought for me that day. Wow, that was twelve years ago. He was my best friend then, and I so badly want to know if he still is and that I can trust him, like I could back then. I know we love each other, we always have I guess, but can I trust him now? He finally breaks the silence.

Paxy, do you want to go to Tombstone? We could just walk around, maybe find that little park that we used to go to, and play catch for a couple of hours, just so that we had an excuse to spend time alone. Do you remember that?

Joey of course I remember. I remember everything about us back then, we were best friends.

Yes we were baby doll.

Joey, I am not going to insult either of us by asking you if you know a Travis Gary from Annapolis. Instead I just want you to tell me how you know him. Also, what is your relationship with Christos Artino?

He looks over at me with a sad look in his eyes. Then he takes in a deep breath, lets it out, and then another just like it, as if, he is trying to find enough oxygen in the car, to speak.

Paxy, I want to be honest with you so I will tell you everything that I can; however, please, please believe me when I tell you there are going to be things that I cannot share, or it will jeopardize many lives, and the biggest case of my career.

Joey, is what brings you back to Bisbee, a case? If so, where do I fit in? I don't understand, are you using me in something, and what we shared last night, was that just part of the deal for your career.

Damn-it Paxy are you kidding me, how could you ever say or even think that?

Well hell Joey I say in a loud angry voice, let me see, I have not heard from you in years yet I am pretty sure that your mom, or someone that we both know has told you way before now that I moved back to Bisbee, and opened up a Gallery called the Brickstone. Now one day this mysterious Private Investigator, from Virginia Mr. Christos Artino wants my help in solving art fraud cases. Then on another day not long after that this suave rich art dealer named Travis Gary from Maryland comes all the way, to a small Gallery in Bisbee Arizona, to purchase more art than I would probably sell in the next six months. Oh, but you already know all of that because the art dealer, Mr. Gary, carries with him your FBI card, along with Mr. Artino's card, in a small folder that he mistakenly dropped in the Brickstone.

Baby Doll, I want to explain all of this if you will calm down and give me a chance.

Please drop the baby doll, I am not a young teenage girl who hangs on your every word anymore. You will do well to remember that when you are explaining all of these coincidences.

Paxy, why did you sleep with me last night? Seems like you have a lot of built up anger where I am concerned.

Maybe it is because I felt like it might be the only time it would ever happen for us given the present day circumstances.

Boy you really do not trust me, do you Paxy?

Not yet, so start spilling your guts, I am listening.

Paxy, as I said I will tell you everything that I can. Please let me say everything without you getting angry, or interrupting with questions. When I finish it is your turn, and you can interrogate me all you want.

Well then maybe we should have just driven to Myranda's office so I could have asked her to do my interrogating for me. After all she is my attorney.

Very cute, Paxy!

Wasn't meant to be cute, just truthful. I have worked hard for everything that I have, and I am not risking it for something I wanted nothing to do with, I am sure of that.

Okay since it is a beautiful day and we are here at the park, let's get out the car for some fresh air, and a walk.

For about thirty seconds we walk, side by side, with neither of us saying a word. Then Joey begins.

Paxy, first of all you are not a pawn in some police case, well not really. Hey, I saw that look and roll of the eyes. Please just give me a fair chance here. Also, lip biting is not allowed. I want those lips to stay as perfect as everything else on your beautiful body.

Flattery will get you nowhere at this moment, just keep talking.

It is true I know both of these men Mr. Gary works for the DEA (Drug Enforcement Administration), and Mr. Artino is a private investigator who works exclusively for me, only in undercover situations. He is employed by the agency, as I am, where they do the hiring, and firing, if you screw up. He only does undercover work. Which is why the first time you met him in Williamsburg everything was done so secretively. Of course, before then, everything was done over the telephone just to offer you some small opportunities that we were sure with your knowledge of art you would handle beautifully, as you did. Those opportunities would hopefully peak your interest in doing something much bigger. When the time was right, something bigger needed to be discussed in person, but of course that discussion could not be with me. We booked you at that little cottage to give off the appearance of someone on a short weekend trip wanting some R&R. This was just a precaution.

He works for you directly? You mean you are the employer that he and the driver in Virginia were referring too? Does he know about our past? That we grew up together?

Yes, he does. He works for me because he is the best at everything he does. Paxy, we both love Bisbee with all of our hearts, and we should, as you said, we grew up here together. Bisbee is I believe the best place there is to enjoy all that is important in a person's life. Especially today with its vibrant new liberal culture. However, a very dark case here in Bisbee has brought me back home, I am sad to say. I should also, say that I was hopeful that you would never have to know what was happening until it was all over. I will share only what I can with you about this case, and then leave it all up to you to believe, and trust in me. Knowing you the way that I hope I do, I believe that I can trust you to keep absolutely everything I share with you, to yourself. Lives could depend on that. Which means not even Myranda can know what I share with you, even as your attorney, or good friend. It has to be as it always was with us when we could share our deepest most personal secrets. Promise me you understand the importance of this.

Okay Joey, I understand. I promise secrecy if it truly is that important.

It is. Okay, first obviously I am not actually taking a leave of absence from the agency. I am working undercover while I am here. Not even my family knows this.

Please just one thing, tell me that you are not investigating anything that may have happened at the Brickstone.

I am not, you can believe that. However, I need to use the Brickstone as a cover just so that my people will have a reason to be known or seen, in Bisbee. Also, it was the perfect choice, because I knew that if anything were to possibly get "compromised," in any way, I could trust you, or at least I hoped I could. It took a whole lot of talking to convince the agency of that fact. I was sure with our shared past that you would keep our undercover operation a secret even if we had to come clean, with you, on how the Brickstone was being used as a cover. I just did not think that it would be so soon that we would be having this conversation. I wanted you to only believe that my leave of absence was about you, and my family. Some R&R for me! How you became suspicious of this is not how I wanted you to find out, believe me.

Keep talking, I am still listening.

Christos Artino does various jobs for me. Enough work that he works, as I told you, solely under me in the agency. Part of his job, this time, was and is, to help me protect you from any of this affecting you personally, or affecting the Brickstone in any adverse way. The job in Rome is a legitimate felony case he is also working on for me. While you were there he was in Bisbee doing a little early undercover work, mainly at the Brickstone. Paxy, there is no easy way to tell you this so I will just come out and say it, the Brickstone is where the (NSID) will do there sting operation, that will lead to several arrests in Bisbee. So now that Christos and yourself, do business together, and you have become friends, of sort, he can be in Bisbee without any suspicion, except of course that maybe I am not the only one in town that wants you for himself. By the way, I told him that I would kill him, myself, if he made any kind of real passes towards you, and he knew that I meant it. So he too will be arriving in Bisbee soon. His first order of business will be to talk to you about your returning trip to Rome. He and I will then meet for the first time, of course. While he is here he will make the decision to spend some time in the area because he has some vacation time, he wants to take. So understandably he wants to see a little more of Southern Arizona, which in reality, will be in Mexico where there are other people that are connected to this case. Both on the side of the law, and not on the side of the law. When the "big sting," takes place, you will be back in Rome finishing things up there, and away from what will be, very ugly, and public. Mr. Gary, who is also going to be working here, comes back because he has other wealthy clients that want the style of art found only in Bisbee, and the surrounding areas. Paxy I realize that you are angry that this was all done without you being in the loop, of knowing what was taking place, but for good reason, that being your safety. There will still be no danger to you if you just trust me to do my job, and you go about your everyday life at the Brickstone before you leave for Rome. Our plan depends on you being away from the Brickstone. So sorry, but I cannot share anymore details with you until the case is closed.

Joey will we be seeing each other while you are here working?

Of course, everything needs to appear normal, and I can't think of anything more normal than you and I being together.

Am I allowed to at least know what and who the case involves, in Bisbee?

No, absolutely not.

Well it definitely must be big if you are here all the way from Washington with two other undercover agents.

Big enough, Murder and Drugs! A cartel that should have been shut down many years ago.

Joey, this is so much to take in, but I am trying to understand. You just need to give me some time to absorb all of it. Hopefully, by the time you get back from Washington I will be better with everything you have told me.

Remember Paxy no one can know, not even Myranda. One word to anyone, and the consequences could be devastating to a lot of people. I mean this, no one.

What about your parents won't they be suspicious of your leave of absence?

Probably, a little. That is another reason that everything has to seem completely normal especially with you and I. I told them that my leave of absence was due to all of the overtime hours with days of non-stop work that I have built up. Also, told them that I need to breathe some small town fresh air for a while to bring back some needed balance in my life.

Joey, I'm sure that there is nothing that would make them happier than for you to decide to give up Washington, and come back to Bisbee to take a permanent position with your dad, and Frank Jr, in the Gems business.

Exactly, but their plan for me to do that is still in the future not right now, but that is complicated too. Another conversation you and I will need to have one day.

Chapter Eleven

Joey and I spend as much time together the next couple of weeks, before he goes back to Washington, as we can squeeze in with my time at the Brickstone, and his time with family commitments. Together we found time to go out for drinks, and dinner with his parents one evening, and on another evening we had dinner together at the family manor with his parents, also his brother Frances (Frank Jr.), and his wife Rose, along with their twin daughters, Carina and Ciana whose seventh birthday we were celebrating.

Myranda and Sam had us over a couple of times for small backyard barbeques, and pool parties. Those evenings were the best where we all reminisced about growing up here. We talked and laughed about all of the crazy things we did, and lived through somehow. Along with all the fun times, and things that happened across the street, from where she and Sam now live. A ball park that played such an important part in all of our lives, memories that we will all cherish forever. They live in Warren, a small suburb on the

lower south end of Bisbee, they have a beautiful home on the popular historic "Vista Park," which is located just across the street to the historic "Warren Ball Park," that has been used as a sports facility since 1909.

Many baseball legends have hit the ball in this park. The ball park was a popular place for traveling teams to play. On November 7th, 1913 the ball park made history when the New York Giants played the Chicago White Sox in a post-season game as the two teams made their way around the world by steamship. This celebrated tour received continuous press coverage throughout 1913-1914. Major League teams, that regularly played exhibition games here in the 1910s, 20s, 30s, and 40s, are the Chicago Cubs, White Sox, Pittsburgh Pirates, New York Giants, Cleveland Indians, and Philadelphia Athletics. Some of the most notable figures in baseball ever to play the game have stepped out onto this field with hopes to one day make it to the big leagues. In the 1920's, some of the "Outlaw" players, implicated in the 1919 "Black Sox" scandal, played here as visiting teams playing against Bisbee teams. Also here, on this historic field, history was made when baseball legends like John McGraw, Connie Mack, and Charlie Comiskey brought their teams, to play here. Many other baseball legends managed or played on this field such as Billy Martin, Charlie Metro, Frank Lucchesi, Clint Courtney, and Earl Williams. Several managers or players started their careers here, or came back to manage at the Warren Ball Park. You know I think if I ever decide to sell the Brickstone I could just become a historian tour guide for Bisbee.

Hello, this is Myranda, and you know I hate talking to your machine. Especially when I know that due to the hour and you're not so active social schedule that you probably are home alone reading your design mags or doing yoga, just choosing not to answer the phone. Call me soon, please.

I call her back the next morning. Since Joey is back in Washington, Myranda assumes that there is nothing of social importance on my calendar. She wants me to make an appointment with her secretary to come in and talk about Travis Gary. I have no idea how to approach this. I have never lied about anything to her, unless of course you count the time that I borrowed a dress out of her closet one weekend before we both left for college when she was out of town with her parents. A dress that she loved more than she loved Sam at the time. I spilled a red grape spritzer on it. I took it to every cleaner in Bisbee, and none of them would touch it, so I threw it away. She always blamed a younger cousin for taking it, and losing it. Her cousin of course continued to deny it. I have promised myself one day I will tell her the truth. Today's conversation though is going to be tough, because it is not about a dress . I am afraid she is going to see right through me. I suggest that we go to lunch somewhere so that we can talk about things. This would be instead of a formal meeting in your office. That way you will not have to charge me your usual three hundred dollars an hour. She laughs, but agrees. I am hoping, maybe she won't grill or push too hard if we are in a public place.

Myranda, I do not want to pursue anything more with Mr. Gary.

I already know that.

What, how could you already know that?

Well one of the persons in the equation, that could probably clear everything up for you, just came back into town for a couple of weeks. During that time I assume that at least some of your pillow talk must have been about Mr. Travis Gary, along with Mr. Christos Artino. I know that you and Joey have stayed pretty busy, so I have not seen much of you other than at the barbecues, and then we were never alone to talk. Plus, you have eaten more of your bottom lip than you have of your Greek salad. I am assuming trying to figure out a way to tell me what is going on. I will tell you right now that all I really want is the entire gossip scoop. After all I am your best friend.

I can barely look at her when I just say, yes. Myranda even though you are my best friend in the world, I promised Joey that I would not say anything to anyone, not even you, whom I tell everything. He said it could put a lot of people in danger if I talk about what has brought him back.

Well at least let me say that I told you those two jackasses were trouble, one of them was just too sexy, and the other just seemed wrong. I know what ever all of this is it has to have something to do with them.

Myranda, I know, and you were right, it seems that I was clueless. Sometimes I feel like I am so worldly then something always happens to humble me. The silver lining though is that I have definitely learned not to accept what I believe to be true of a person until they have proven themselves to me first.

When can you share everything with me? You know that not just the friend in me, but the attorney in me makes me suspicious of everything, so I am dying to know it all.

I know you are, and I am dying to tell you all of it, or at least the little bit that he could tell me, which was very little, but I promised not to. I am afraid we are both going to have to wait to know everything about this "situation," for lack of a better term to call it, until it is over. The problem is I have no idea when that might be, he couldn't even tell me that.

Paxy, please at least tell me if either of those jackasses involve you in something illegal?

No, they definitely did not. Can we just change the subject?

Sure, so tell me about you and Joey. That is the other thing that I have been dying to know ever since the two of you were at the house, and he casually drops, that he is taking a leave of absence to spend time here in Bisbee.

Myranda, I was just as shocked as you were when he told me about the leave of absence. He just has so much overtime earned that I guess this is a good time for him to take a vacation, rather than take the money for it. Also, I really hope part of it is that he wants to spend time with me.

It is pretty obvious that while he is here that the two of you will be together, but what about when he goes back. Long distance relationships are hell, from what I hear about them, and Washington is a long commute to Bisbee, my friend.

Myranda, I have no idea we did not touch on that subject. We did talk about denying our love for each other in high school but, agreed that we both needed to leave Bisbee to go out in to the world so we could see other people, do other things, and just grow up. I know I had to go spread my wings for a while, and as the saying goes: if it was meant to be those same wings would carry me back here to Bisbee. I needed to be gone for the time that I was especially after my parent's car accident. All I know for sure, at this very moment, is that there is no reason for Joey and I to look back at what might have been. When now there could be so much in front of us. Myranda, I love that man like crazy. I have butterflies in my stomach, and starbursts in my soul.

Sweet Paxy, my dearest friend, you always did when you were around him, but back then you just really never understood the meaning of it all.

Chapter Twelve

Joey is due back today. We have talked on the phone every night since he left, two weeks ago. We are like two teenagers getting to know each other for the first time, except that we already have a history. I think I even like the older version of him better. His face has only changed, to be somewhat fuller, still has that sexy five-o'clock shadow look, at the end of every day, even though he shaves every morning. He has that rough and ripped look to him like a man in a uniform should have. I know this I have not had such a spontaneous and sensual reaction to a man in .....Ever!

Jillie I want to talk to you this morning when you get back from making the bank deposit.

Sure Paxy, is everything okay?

Definitely, just something that I want to share with you, no big thing. Of course as I am saying this to her I am thinking to myself, no big thing just maybe one of the biggest busts that has ever happened in Bisbee in my lifetime. Also, I have no details of who, or when; however, I gave permission for it to take place, whenever, in the Brickstone where you and I make our living. Surely they won't shoot up or burn down my Gallery. Shit-O Friday, what have I done? Hopefully, I can write this in my journal one day as just another strange adventure in the life and times of Paxton Steele. Okay, I have to clear my head, all at once the Brickstone seems to be full of customers, and Jillie is at the bank. Seems like it is really busy for a Tuesday morning, but I am not complaining.

Good morning Paxton how are you today?

Just fine Mrs. Lowell, can I help you with something special this morning?

I am hoping to find a truly special wedding gift for my granddaughter, Rhonda. She and Casey Brandt are going to be married next month. Of course they have lived together for almost ten years so they have everything they need. I want something that they do not know that they need, until I give it to them. I thought that the Brickstone would be the perfect place to look with all of your art pieces. I like the fact that everything in here is one of a kind original, not going to be a reproduction of some sort. With Casey being an art appraiser I thought they would appreciate a new piece of art for their home. You know I'm not one to brag; however, he makes a pretty decent living here in Bisbee. We have a lot of art lovers, in our community. Who would have ever guessed that fifty years ago? We were just a mining town back in my youth. But everything has changed today, and I think I like it better this way. Even for an old women like myself there is a great deal of diversity of things to see, and do. You know I hope I never get too old to mix things up a little bit. Bisbee is a good place to keep a heart young.

Mrs. Lowell since you have lived here your entire life, I think that I have something that may interest you. Now I am not sure if Rhonda and Casey would like it, but I feel it would make a wonderful wedding gift for someone that has everything else that they need.

That is what I want to see, so let's have a look at whatever you are talking about.

She stares at the paintings of Bisbee that I show her from various artists with this long lazy pause not saying a word. It is like she is looking at a place she has never seen before. It took some getting used to when I first came back to the relaxed slower pace that people seem to make the normal here, but I like it, a lot. Finally she speaks, I will take two, one for a wedding gift, and one for my living room. I really don't need one, but I think I want one.

Well Mrs. Lowell you are talking to an expert in the area of needing and wanting. I like to think that if you want something bad enough then you absolutely need it!

Paxton I like you, please call me Julie. Now I need your help in picking out which ones I should get. I like that they are all different views of Bisbee, and all in different frames.

Okay, well one of my favorites is this panoramic with the beautiful sunset, and one of my other favorites is this one that has all of the light colored hues of blues and mauves that shows the "B," on the hill.

Paxton, you have sold me, do you do wedding wrap?

Of course which painting would you like me to wrap for Rhonda and Casey?

I think the one with the "B."

Perfect, if you have any other shopping you would like to do, I have a few more customers I should help then I will get right on it. I could have it for you in about an hour, if that will work for you.

That will be just great, see you in about an hour. Paxton, you are a sweetheart, and the Brickstone is lovely. It is hard to imagine how a sweet, young, and beautiful thing like you is still single.

I laugh? Well I guess it is just another one of those mysteries in this thing we call life.

She then gives me a wink, and says, maybe not a mystery, maybe you are just picky, and waiting for the right man. I heard that Joseph Dalecki is back in Bisbee, for a time, just a rumor mind you. But, if memory serves me correctly the two of you had a very close friendship before you both left for college.

She then turns and walks out the door. Hmm....yes indeed I think to myself, the rumor mill is alive and well in this small town we live in. I then start helping other customers for about the next half hour.

Paxy, I am back from the bank along with the other errands that needed done Jillie says when she walks in. So just let me know when you have time for that visit.

Thanks, now is good. We can talk privately out here, since all is quiet, and I can wrap this wedding present while we visit.

Jillie, I know what I am going to tell you will sound crazy, but please trust me when I say that everything is going to be okay. I just need you to not ask me any questions, right now, in regards to what I found out about Mr. Artino, and Mr. Gary. There definitely will be a time that all of your questions will be answered, and sooner than later, I hope. Also, you are going to have an opportunity to meet Mr. Artino as he and Mr. Gary will both be in and out of Bisbee, and the Brickstone, in the near future.

Paxy, I have to say that I am confused, and a whole lot curious.

Yet, I trust you completely as my employer because, I know how much the Brickstone means to you, and I trust you, in my heart, because you are the dearest friend that I have here in Bisbee.

Thank you, Jillie!

Later that day, when Jillie goes home for the day, I stay for just a little longer to work on some paperwork, then I go upstairs. I check the locks twice, make sure the low lights that I leave on during the night hours are adjusted correctly, and then double check that the alarm is set. Lately I have become somewhat paranoid. I want to do my yoga, then take a bath before Joey gets here. When I spoke to him earlier he said he would be here at about ten, so I have three hours. He drove the thirty three hours, to get here, instead of flying to Tucson, or Phoenix, then getting a car that the agency would rent for him. He said that he wanted to drive, because he had never taken the time before now to do that. He was looking forward to a few days, to himself, to think about a lot of things that he needed to sort out in his head. Also, was looking forward to the road trip in his Jaguar.

Chapter Thirteen

As Joey and I start undressing each other, I start to unbutton his shirt when I see that he has a black Glock 9 millimeter pistol in a leather thong holster wrapped diagonally down his chest, and onto his side under his left arm. He puts his finger to my mouth, and whispers not now. He removes the holster, along with the gun himself, and lays it on my nightstand. Then gently he lays me down onto the bed as we continue to undress each other. I feel like I am being devoured with his kiss. We both have a fiery hunger for each other, as he knows just where I need to be touched. He takes a long slow journey down my bare back with his kisses then with great ease flips me over, to come back up to my mouth for another taste. This time our kisses are deeper with pleasure. We spend the next few hours with our naked bodies entangled, and pleasuring each other.

Morning comes quickly, and we both have things to do. He needs to go to the compound after breakfast, and I need to go to the Brickstone.

I have thought so much about the two of us while I was back in Washington. I do not want this to sound corny. I just want you to know how deep my feelings are for you. Two weeks ago, when I walked up behind you, on the veranda, I felt my legs almost go week. It felt like all of my blood was rushing from my body. I mean it, I could not wait to have you turn around so that I could look into your beautiful eyes. I was hoping that when you looked, back at me, that there would be that same wanting in them as I know you must have seen in mine. Even though I tried so hard to play it cool. I wanted you at that very moment more than I have ever wanted anything, or any woman before. Now, I believe that we both felt that want, especially when you leaned into me for that kiss.

Joey, there is no denying that I want you. Life is so complicated right now with the real reason why you are here along with the lies that we are telling people, or at least the half-truths we are telling. My heart says that everything will be fine in the end, but my emotions are in conflict with that. I am damn scared. I have everything to lose, including you, when you have to go back to Washington. You have nothing to lose, unless you are not able to close this mysterious case that has brought you back here in the first place. I know that you cannot give me details; however, it is so strange that an important (NSID) agent from Washington DC would be needed on a case in his small hometown in Arizona. I have spent some time on the computer looking at some of the cases that you have been involved in, and I can't imagine that anything going on in Bisbee could be of that importance. My imagination is on overdrive Joey.

I am so sorry. This case is definitely going to blind side many people in this community. There is no one though, that it is going to affect, or be any harder on, than me. Because this is my hometown, and I love it here as much as you do. Somedays when I over think it, I would give anything to not be the one that has to make this criminal bust. For reasons though that I cannot share at this time. I am the one that can finally make it happen before more lives are taken, or at the very least, ruined. Believe me though, because it is here in Bisbee there were lots of hours spent with the agency trying to figure out another way. The facts are though that it is going to be myself and my team that brings this cartel down. In some other unexplainable kind of way it also makes me proud to be the one that will be responsible for stopping these ruthless gangsters. Since I know something about these people, along with this community, there is a much better chance of less blood shed with me being in charge.

Joey, what about our local police department, are they aware of what is happening?

Yes, of course. They have been in on every stage of the planning strategy from the very beginning, almost eighteen months now.

Are you sure that you are going to be safe?

In a not so convincing laugh in his voice, he tells me that I worry too much. I get up from the table, to place my plate in the sink, and once again most of my breakfast, that he made, still on it. My appetite seems to leave me every time we have this similar conversation. From the sink I look back over my shoulder at him, and tell him that I am not sure that I can pull off this act, that nothing is wrong. I wish that I did not have to know any of this, and that myself and the Brickstone, did not have to be a part of it. I feel like I am a pawn in a chess game that is waiting to be removed.

Paxy now you are just plain acting crazy. I would never put you in any type of direct danger. The only reason that I chose the Brickstone, for the perfect place, is that you are so trusted, and well respected in the community, and the players will never suspect.

Remember you promised to trust me to do my job. In doing that

I would never let anything happen to you because you are the most important thing in the world to me. You are like a part of me, since you were about eleven. So give me a smile, and a kiss, because I have to leave. I will check in with you later so we can make dinner plans. I want to take you somewhere special so I can spoil you, baby doll. Trust me, everything will end up being fine, I promise!

Chapter Fourteen

For the next few weeks' things seemed to be going along pretty normally considering the circumstances that were surrounding my life. Joey moved into the manor, we saw each other every chance that we could. We talked about how much easier our relationship made his life, while he was working on this case. Because he was able to say that he was spending him time with me when he was actually working. I can truthfully say that I am excited that I will be going back to Rome soon, hopefully to find out from the Bishop Nick that the two paintings that were taken are original Sandro Botticelli's. My attitude towards what Joey and his men are doing, is much better with every day that passes. We have an agreement not to talk about the case any more than we just have too. Christos has taken me to lunch a couple of times for appearance sake. We have even laughed some about how nervous and suspicious I was when we met for the first time in Williamsburg.

He said that he felt like a failure for the first time in his life as an undercover agent. He had completely underestimated me, and how hard it would be to sell me on the job. Then laughing he said, meeting you to talk about the job that would take you to Rome was supposed to be the easy part. I think that I was somewhat hoodwinked, with that one, by the boss man.

Probably!

Myranda and I seem to find more time to get together these days. She seems to have a need to keep up with everything happening in my life, and to know for sure that I am okay. She isn't buying the story anymore that Joey is just on a long deserved vacation. She tells me that there has been an arrest in the Laura Pilner murder case. It apparently had something to do with an ongoing drug case. Seems that her murder may have been a vendetta against Ray Oliver her boyfriend who is an Arizona Border Patrol Officer. The suspect is thought to have ties to an Arizona cartel.

Hmm, Myranda that is crazy! Do they think there are members of this cartel that live in Bisbee?

Paxy, I assume they do, and that is why Ray Oliver is involved. Probably a Mexico-Arizona Cartel that has been around for years. Some of these cartels have been around for decades of family generations. Do you think this case may be part of what has brought Joey here from Washington?

I have no idea, and I choose not to think about it right now. I do not want to jinx the special evening that Joey and I have planned. The first evening in a long time that he is not working. We are planning dinner, a movie, then back to my apartment for the night. I am going to wear the summer white cotton mini dress with the short yellow top jacket that I bought, when you and I went to Tucson, shopping, a few months ago. My first time to wear it, I was saving it for something special. I am hoping that when we get back to my place tonight, I can find a way to bring up the subject of, what happens to us after he goes back to

Washington.

I am happy to know that you are at least acknowledging this could be a problem. It is about time the two of you talk about that. Surely he knows that you have to live here, full time, with the Brickstone.

Exactly, but it is not like his career is unimportant with what he does in Washington. It is just something that I think we need to start thinking about. His mother even asked me the same thing last Saturday when she, Rose, and I were fixing lunch, while Frank, Frank Jr., and Joey were in Frank's office discussing family business.

Asked you what?

If Joey and I had discussed what our future might be when he is back in Washington.

That had to be awkward, what did you say?

The truth, we have not talked about it. I can never tell though what Charlotte is thinking. I feel like she approves of Joey and me, but one never knows.

Paxy, too bad if she doesn't. The two of you are adults, and what you decide is really none of her business.

You would think that; however, I have the impression, that everything that her boys do, she makes it her business. Family business is what the Dalecki's are all about.

Paxy, before you leave to get ready for your night with Joey, I have been wanting to have you tell me about the compound, and what it looks like all these years later. I have not been near the Dalecki Manor, in years. I am not sure that I can even remember what it ever looked like. I just never have a reason to be up on the high divide road where the manor is.

Myranda, there is no denying that the Dalecki manor truly is beautiful. It seems somehow to have a certain mystique, and at the same time is feels to me to have a lurking danger about it that I cannot ever explain. It is certainly one of the stateliest, and most magnificent homes in old upper Bisbee. It has the look of a palace encircled with beautiful flowers and statues. Even its ten foot high black decorative iron scrolled fence with beautiful roses and ivy vines that help keep the manor secluded for privacy is incredibly beautiful. Then there are the black iron gates to the driveway of the property that are adorned with detailed sculptured gargoyles at each side. When you drive through the gates there is a twenty foot cherub fountain all lit up in the center of a large circle drive in front of the manor. The driveway is all done with dark Charcoal Grey pavers. The manor its self is built with light colored Heather Grey bricks, and stone. The trim is all done in a satin luster black.

Paxy, I can't remember is it two or three stories tall?

It is four stories. The main floor has an entry parlor, formal dining room, a great room with a Cherrywood built in bar, and a kitchen with a breakfast nook with bowed windows from floor to ceiling. Through beautiful double French doors from the great room you walk out to an incredible garden of perennial and wild flowers, on the west side of the home. Charlotte said that the caretakers are diligent to make sure that there are fresh flowers in the manor from the garden, at all times. There is a master bedroom suite with bath, along with two more full bathrooms on the main floor. The office is also, on the main floor. The office is my favorite room in the entire home. It has two walls that are completely of the original brick, and is furnished with all deep red soft Italian leather sofas and chairs. There is an enormous antique Cherrywood desk with a high back matching chair in the same red leather. On the west wall it has an end to end magnificent fireplace built with rare rock stones that were imported from South Africa. The last wall is an all Cherrywood bookcase, with a Sycamore wood ladder, that slides from one end of the bookcase to the other. The bookcase shelves are full with beautiful books, some are original leather bound documentaries. There are also, family pictures of many generations of Dalecki's, in beautiful and one of a kind frames, arranged through out the shelves among the books. Then going up to the second floor from the back of the great room, there is a beautiful Cherrywood grand curved staircase.

Paxy, it sounds exquisite! To think I have always thought of it being creepy and possibly even haunted.

My friend you know me, I think it is quite probably haunted. Especially the two middle floors. Whenever you are on either of those floors, the lace curtains seem to be rustling in the wind, even when the windows are closed, and there is no wind blowing outside. Both floors have a romantic feel to them partly due to the beautiful floral wallpaper, and also, that partly comes from what seems to be a hint of Jasmine without the help of flowers or candles. The scent is subtle, but distinctive. These two floors are my very favorite, and I swear I have seen dark shadows in some of the wall mirrors that look like outlines of very old people that are all wearing hats. Immediately after you climb to the second, or third floor you start to feel a presence of people that are not visible, except for an instant in an old mirror if you are lucky. Oh-Yeah, I am telling you those two floors are haunted, no doubt about it. I have told Joey this, and he says that his family has always felt that the whole home was haunted by the Dalecki ancestors who built it a century ago. He says that there are not only the outlines of ancestors which they have look-a-like old photos of, but there has always been unexplained echoes throughout the home. It is like the echoes are trying to communicate, but the family long ago learned to ignore the sounds. When Joey and I were kids he told me a story that at the time he made me promise not to share with anyone. His story was about one of the bedrooms on the third floor, south side. When his grandparents were much older, his grandfather used that bedroom, and his grandmother used the north side bedroom. It was that way for the last few years of his their lives together on this earth. Joey's bedroom was on the second floor right below his grandfather's. After his grandparents were both gone, Joey would sometimes go up to the third floor, and play, or study in the room that was once his grandfather's. He liked the scent that always seemed to be permeating in the room. It was the scent of a cigar, and it reminded him of his grandfather, and how close they were. Sometimes without ever telling anyone he would even sleep in that bedroom instead of his own, it always made him feel safe, he said. The interesting fact though that made Joey believe that it must be his grandfather's ghost was that his grandfather never smoked his cigars anywhere but in the garden. No one was ever allowed to smoke inside the home. We talked about this again just the other day, and he says now though when he goes into that room the scent seems to be much more diluted or faint, but that is the room he stays in when he is visiting. One more thing that I have heard the family speak of regarding those two floors, it that there is a mystery of why those floors never have any dust in them, or on anything in any of their rooms. Lastly these two floors on the inside have had very little remodeling, but are in as good of condition as the rest of the manor that has been restored. Rose and I were talking just the other day about this very thing. She said the caretakers never spend time on those two floors unless ordered to by Charlotte because they are expecting many overnight guests. Charlotte was laughing when she told Rose that she once has caught them opening all of the outside doors and windows while they were burning sage smudges to get rid of all the paranormal activity.

Okay, I think I have heard enough about it being haunted. No damn wonder I have always felt that compound was so damn unnerving. And no wonder you have always had a strange feeling regarding Joey's family. But, I do enjoy hearing all about the elegant décor, so just continue with that.

Well then, before we completely leave these two floors just let me tell you of their beautiful décor. They both have Victorian furnished landings off of the elegant Cherrywood grand staircases that wishbone out to both sides of each floor. There are four bedrooms on each floor with private baths to each.

Paxy, there of course is a fourth floor so let's move on to it.

Of Course, where else would they have room to entertain their large balls and gala's? This floor also, comes up from another grand curved Cherrywood staircase that opens up to another large great room that is identical to the great room on the main level only this room has a bar that takes up one entire wall. The floors on the entire fourth level are all sycamore wood that contrasts beautifully with the staircase. This is the only wood flooring in the manor. The rest of the manor has a thick blue-gray carpet and gray slate flooring throughout. Off of this great room is a large kitchen, then there are two more bathrooms.

What about the grounds outside?

Absolutely gorgeous. There is an expansive green back yard that has a pool, with a separate building that is the pool house. It that has two showers, a changing room with rose marble vanities, a dry sauna, a wet bar that is always fully stocked I imagine, and green and rose lounging sofas. Then away from that in what I would guess, to be about a hundred yards back, tucked away in a private little oasis of its own. There is a small forest of large old cottonwood trees, along with beautiful Arizona mesquite trees that surround the red brick caretaker's home, where the Pacheco's reside. The entire manor estate is surround by the black fencing that you can see from the road.

Paxy, you know that the Christmas party, that the Dalecki's host every year, is invitation only, and known to be the group of political bigwigs, of who's who in Arizona. You my friend just might be on that list this year if you stay in the good graces of the family.

Or maybe not, if Joey is not here.

Chapter Fifteen

Joey and I leave my apartment at just about dusk with the sky still having that twilight glow that it sometimes gets right before a threatening monsoon rainstorm. One of my favorite times of day, and year. The other being of course just before the dawn of early morning when the sky is cracking with thunder during a monsoon. The warm air tonight, and the beautiful colors of the Arizona sunset are just perfect for what I hope is going to be our most memorable night together, so far. Dinner, a movie, and then back to my apartment for the evening, maybe some wine, along with a long soak in the claw foot tub before bed. After we are in the Jaguar Joey turns to me, and says you look stunning tonight. He takes a small box from the pocket of his casual dress jacket. I find myself staring at a beautiful teardrop pendent bright Sapphire necklace that hangs from two delicate chains that sparkle with little diamonds like dew drops.

Joey, thank you for being so loving, but most of all for being the kind of man I can love.

Stroking my face lightly with his hand he tells me that he hopes he can always be the kind of man that I deserve.

Joey, I want this night to be a night for just us that we will both remember when we are old. It almost feels too good to be true that we are finally together again, only in a romantic relationship.

Paxy, me too. You were all that I could think about while I was back in Washington, which believe me was not good for the paperwork that was piled up, and waiting for me when I got there.

Paxy my love, we do need to make one quick stop at a man's home, named Marc Ricco, before our dinner reservations. Then I promise the night is all ours. It is only going to take a few minutes, I promise. He has some documents that I asked him to get for me. I want to pick them up tonight, before the weekend begins. If you are comfortable with this, it will probably be quicker if you wait in the car for me. That way we can avoid introductions, and small talk.

When we pull up and park in front of Marc Ricco's home, with the top to the Jaguar down, we can hear music coming from the back of the home. Just before Joey gets out of the car he says to me I am going to put the top back up, and I want you to keep the doors closed while I am gone. Then he gives me a big smile and a sexy wink. I watch him walk to the front door and ring the doorbell. He stands there for about thirty seconds before he rings the bell again. After no one comes to the door within about thirty more seconds, he starts to walk around the home to where the music is playing. I sit in the car, for about fifteen minutes, before I start getting angry, thinking we are going to miss our dinner reservation at San Pellegrino's. I starved myself all day so that I could enjoy the great Italian cuisine that they serve. I cannot hear any voices coming from the back of the home, or hear anything coming from inside the home. All of the window coverings are closed but, there seems to be some soft lighting on inside the home. Now a black Lincoln pulls up in front of an empty lot across the street. It is dark enough now that I cannot see who is in the car but, I think the windows might be tinted anyway. No one gets out of the car. This plus still no sight of Joey is making me very nervous. I set there for about five more minutes then decide to go see what is keeping him. A loud voice coming from the Lincoln yells at me.

Hey sexy lady if you see Ricco in there tell him his ride is here, please.

I don't even turn around. I just keep walking towards the back of the home like I know exactly what I am doing and where I am going. In reality I am having a hard time seeing much of anything; however, I can still follow the music that has continued to blast this entire time. There is a boom-box setting on the concrete of the covered patio behind the home. There is a large patio-table with food and drinks still on it, and maybe a dozen chairs here, but no one is around. I go to the back door and knock, but no one answers. I get the feeling someone is moving around inside. Now I am too scared to walk back to the jag. I walk just a few feet more going away from the back of the patio, to the edge of the desert. I hide behind some sage bush, and tall cactus. Trying to figure out the muffled noises coming from the desert, it is hard to make out exactly what the sounds are because of the boom-box music that is blaring behind me. Now with no warning at all. I hear the sound of what seems like hundreds of gunshots cracking like thunder bolts somewhere out in front of me. I scream loud before I can stop myself, and almost pee myself. I crouch down even lower, pull my legs up close to my chest with my arms wrapped around them. My face is buried behind my knees, and I am trying not to scream again, or make any noise. The gunshots continue for only a few more seconds. Then the desert seems to be completely soundless. Not knowing for sure where Joey is, or if he was a part of all of the shooting, all I know is that I am afraid for not just him but, my life as well. I cannot make myself get up to run. I feel paralyzed with my terror. The only thing that I am aware of for sure is the non-stop ringing in my ears. I am wondering if my body has gone into some type of shock. Maybe, I have been shot, and I am dying. Damn it, why can't I move? Then out of nowhere a large hand, coming from behind me, covers my mouth.

Quiet, it is me, Joey!

It is him, I recognize his voice immediately.

He slowly moves his hand from my mouth, and wraps his large arms around my crouched body. I immediately start crying, but there is no sound coming out, just tears running down my face. He holds me tight like both of our lives might depend it. Then in almost an inaudible very low voice he begins cussing at me. Son-of-bitch, what the bloody hell do you think you are doing disobeying my orders, and getting out of the car. It is damn miracle that you did not get your fool-stupid damn head shot right off of your shoulders. I can't believe that I now have to find a safe way to get the both of us the hell out of here without being seen, or before we both are killed. Damn you, Paxy!

Paxy, we have no choice we have to run for it right now before the shooting starts again. Can you stand up, and hold tight to my hand? But, before I can find my voice to answer due to the shock that I still feel I must be in. He yanks hard on my arm then pulls me around, and up to my feet. Somehow, I still feel nothing; however, we are both running, or he is dragging me.

We get back to the Jaguar. Joey floors the gas so that we tear out of there like a bolt of lightning, as we are speeding by the street lamps, in this small neighborhood, they all look like miniature flashing bulbs. We slow down as we get closer to the manor up on the divide. He turns onto a small gravel road that goes through an open gate on the back side about fifty yards from his family's caretaker's brick home. He stops the car, and turns the headlights out. It is pitch black in the car, and I have not stopped shaking, and tears are still silently coming down my face. I feel like I don't even know this maniac crazy man I am with.

He embraces my face with his large hands, starts wiping the tears away with his thumbs, they feel cold, and rough. I know that we are facing each other as I can feel his breath on my face. He brings my face to his mouth for a quick and tender kiss before he says in his low Italian husky voice, after what you witnessed tonight, I can only hope that I am still a man you want to be with. Being a part of my life with the agency responsibilities is not always going to be easy. That is another reason that I have not let myself get in a serious relationship, or start a family. I knew though that coming back here it would be impossible to resist you, especially if you felt the way I did. I am now even sorrier for deciding we needed to involve you in the way that we did, to make everything go according to our plan. This will probably not be the last time that I have to ask for your forgiveness for the things that happen in my line of work. I promise you though, I will never again have you with me when I am working even if it is to be a non-volatile situation like tonight was supposed to be. Tonight I screwed up because I was thinking that I was going to be doing nothing more than picking up a few information documents that Ricco had for my use on this case. You could have so easily been killed.

I am still shaking, my lips are quivering with terror as I am trying to speak to him. Joey, I do not know what to say, I have never been so scared. But, you are right about one thing, you sure as hell screwed up. What the hell just happed besides us both almost getting killed?

Paxy, I understand you are terrified. There is nothing more important right now though than making sure you are safe. We don't really have any more time to discuss, or waste sitting here. I only pulled off to let you calm down some so that I could explain that we need to go to an appointed "safe house property" where

we are going to spend the night. It is just a pre-caution. I can't leave you alone after what just happened, I may not be the only one that knows you were out there.

Joey, what I want to know now, what the hell did just happen?

Paxy, I promise that we will talk about it when I find out exactly what the hell happened, and what went so wrong. Sometimes when working on the Drug and Weapons Special Task Force you are put in the middle of war, that can bring with it bloodshed, and death. Tonight though was a completely unexpected event. I am not even sure of who the good guy's verses the bad guys were. I know it sounds horrible, but things in this country would be a whole hell of a lot worse without the agencies, like the one I work for. Questions right now have to wait, because I have no answers.

I would rather just go back to my apartment if that is okay, and not to your safe house.

Listen to me! We are not going back to your place until I have everything checked out completely, and know that it is safe. Also, we are not able to stay at the manor. Remember my family has no idea that I am working a case while I am here. A hotel for us would cause suspicion, so our only choice is the safe house that is not in use right now. You and I will be the only people there.

Joey, a safe house seems so ominous to me. Can we maybe go stay at Frank Jr. and Rose's home?

No, they have little children that I do not want to scare. Also, they cannot know that I am working a case while I am here.

You mean with all this time that you have been spending with him, and your father working you have nor confided in them with the truth?

Dammit Paxy, telling no one anything, means just that, he screams at me again.

I scream back this time, go to hell Joey. I hate this case, and I hate you too, right now.

He starts the car again, and we leave. We drive to an area in upper Bisbee that is high in the cactus on the hills, and so remote, behind the old high school. The school is the only thing that I recognize, I never knew this place existed, but I guess that is sort of the point to a safe house. After we park his car, in a place that is mostly out of sight unless you know exactly where and what you are looking for, you would never see it. Then we climb at least forty concrete steps to a small little, but handsome house, on the side of the hill, that is hidden behind Mesquite trees, and beautiful Rhododendron bushes.

Chapter Sixteen

There is a key hidden behind a loose brick on the south side of the house that you have to find by fighting your way through a thick patch of Saguaro Cactus. As I watched Joey manipulate his way through the cactus to get the hidden key I feel like turning and running. Maybe, if I did not stop running for a very long time I could somehow outrun this nightmare that I am involved in. But, again my body just feels paralyzed. Mostly now I feel paralyzed with fear that I cannot trust Joey.

Paxy, I am going to take you inside, then I want to return outside to walk around for just a few moments to make myself familiar with the outside of the house.

Have you ever been here before tonight?

No, never!

Then how did you know exactly where to find it, and where to find the key?

That is part of my job, to know these things.

He unlocked, and opened the door. We walk into a small furnished living room that was lit up only by moonlight coming through a high horizontal window. Joey walked over to a lamp that looked like a small barrel cactus, and turned it on for more light. Now, I could see pretty much everything from this one spot in the living room where I was standing. This little house is no more than a one bedroom, one bath, and kitchen home.

Paxy, see if you can find if there is any air-conditioning while I go back outside, please. I will only be a few minutes.

Uh-huh, I have heard that before. Maybe this time you will not be so lucky, you just might get your damn head shot off. We both just stood there and looked at each other. Now for the first time I could not look at him without tears in my eyes that started running down my cheeks. He started to approach me. I held up my hands to motion go, then I said just go do whatever you need to do outside.

Paxy, we are both tired, and emotional. Again, there is so little that I can tell you about what happened tonight that I think we need to try to just get some sleep. Tomorrow morning before I take you back to your apartment I will explain what I can.

Was anyone killed tonight behind Mr. Ricco's home?

Yes, pretty sure at least two of my men, not sure about any others.

Joey, you are right! I do not think that I want to know anything else tonight.

That is the first good thing tonight, Paxy.

The next morning which was probably only about two hours after I had fallen asleep, I woke up to the moonlight now coming into the bedroom window. All at once then the fiasco of everything that happened the night before, and this small little bedroom where I was waking up in this morning everything came rushing back. I remember then Joey is laying behind me. I roll over to look at him. He must feel my stare as he opens his eyes to look back at me. I immediately tense as everything seems so real not to mention massive, and over whelming all at once. Tears immediately well up in my eyes once again.

It's okay Paxy, take a deep breath then let it out slowly, and then just breathe normal. I made you a promise that everything would be okay, and it will be.

Joey this case, does it also, have something to do with how Laura Pilner died?

Yes, and I am sorry about that; however, Laura would have never died if she had listened to us, and went into protective custody. She was in danger just by association of the wrong people. That sometimes is just one of the many in-justices of how cartels work. There are always casualties of innocent people that were just in the wrong place at the wrong time.

You mean like I was last night.

Exactly, and that is the reason that I brought you here instead of taking you home. Like I said, I needed to protect you just in case you were seen by someone else. Did you see anyone else before I came up behind you?

No, I was crouched down, and too scared to look up. One of the reasons though that I left the Jaguar, besides you being gone for so long was that there was a black Lincoln car that came, and parked across the street. I was beginning to get really nervous. No one ever got out, and I could not see who, or how many people were in it. When I was walking towards the house a man yelled for me to tell Ricco that his ride was there.

I will see what I can find out about the black Lincoln. Do you know if the plates were US or Mexico?

That is a good question, I do remember looking at the plates. Then thinking that they were different than any plates that I had ever seen, and I wondered if they were from out of state. The plate had a design that was hard to make out below a line of numbers, there were no letters. The color of the plate was turquoise.

That could be helpful. You wouldn't happen to remember the numbers, would you?

I don't think so. I just remember thinking that it was peculiar that there were only numbers.

That could actually mean several different things; however, the first thing that comes to mind is it was possibly an official government plate of some type.

Joey, who is Marc Ricco?

He was an informant that has been most useful in this case. But, what happened last night tells us that his cover was compromised somehow.

What do you mean was?

He was one of the men shot and killed last night. Paxy, I am sorry that you were there last night to witness any of this. I should have gone by his house before I ever picked you up. Never should I have taken you there with me last night. It can always be dangerous whenever you are dealing with a case, no matter what, where, or when. Also, in my line of work there are no coincidences, last night we were set up. That is one reason that most agents stay single for so long, you never know what might happen next. We get way too good at closing down, and not talking about what we do, or what we see while on the job.

This kind of thing was also, exactly what the agencies concerns were with you and I being so close. I have to be more careful, or I will be the one to compromise the case instead of closing it.

Joey, I have felt from the very beginning that this is more than just a case to you, it is personal. Am I right?

Maybe, but if you ever let a case become too personal that is when things can go wrong. Truthfully it is only personal because it is here in Bisbee. It is just so damn wrong what these people of complete greed get away with. They are money hungry ruthless bastards, and do not care about innocent people that may get in there way. I could not live with myself knowing everything that has now been discovered regarding this particular cartel, if I do not do everything possible to bring them down.

Joey, I am so in love with the good man that you are. But, last night I saw a dark side of you that scares me even more than that bad boy persona did when we were growing up. That is probably why I was always attracted to you back then. There is just something about a bad boy, good man that a girl, or a woman cannot resist. Not to mention how sexy you are even with your messy bed hair this morning, you are so damn irresistible at times. But still, I feel that dark side is something that I should fear.

Well right now I want nothing more than for this irresistible man to take advantage of your hot body; however, we need to leave while it is early, and most likely people are still sleeping. I do not want to draw attention to us that is unnecessary.

I definitely agree with that, besides I have a lot of things at work I need to do this morning. My priority today was going to be getting together with your mother who is ready to look at my suggestions for the new art at the manor. Should I still do that?

Yes, remember normalcy is the best way to handle things. Just stay inside the Brickstone today. Do not leave unless you check in with me first, and I damn well expect you to do what I say from now on. Also, do you care if I use your apartment to take care of business today after I check in with my family at the manor? I have phone calls to make, also I need to see what is out there in chatter about what happened last night. See who all has been assigned to the case now. I need a quiet place for concentration, and limited interruptions. I have a feeling my mother will keep you busy most of the afternoon which is a good thing today. Try not to talk much about last night. We will have to tell anyone that might ask that we decided just to stay in last night. You might want to call this morning to make our apologies about missing our dinner reservation. I hate that kind of thing, I mean just not showing up somewhere that I am expected to be.

I was thinking the same thing, so I will call as soon as they open later today. Joey, yes you can use my apartment today, but I do not want you to spend the night. You can get outside security to make sure things are safe if you want, but I want to be alone tonight. I need to try to figure out the mixed feeling I have about you, or maybe just us.

Paxy, don't overthink this like you do everything else, dammit you make me crazy. I don't have time, or want to deal with your feelings right now, so just let it go. Remember, don't leave the Brickstone today without my permission.

He shuts the door behind him as I am saying: I can't believe that I waited this long in my life to find out that I was in love with a crazy demanding son-of-a-bitch.

Chapter Seventeen

All hell broke out in town last night Paxy, Jillie tells me when I come downstairs from the apartment. Did you hear that there was another shooting in Bisbee last night? I heard that several people were killed. I could hear all kinds of emergency vehicles with their deafening sirens going to whatever was happening from my apartment. To think that one of the things that I fell in love with about Bisbee right from the beginning is how little crime it has.

Jillie, usually there is little crime here. Was there anything in the newspaper about what happened?

Yes, it said there were multiple casualties in a shootout near Naco Highway in the San Jose area of Bisbee. A suspected Cartel Organization Involvement was the headline. The Border Patrol, Bisbee Police, Bisbee Sheriff, along with the CSI, and FBI were all on the scene throughout the night, and are still there this morning. No names were given for any of the casualties. It is of course is the entire front page news this morning.

Joey and I decided to stay in last night. Glad we did, seems we missed all of the excitement.

Really that surprises me. You told me how excited you were about your date with him last night. You even mentioned that you were going to wear your new white lace chiffon sundress.

Well you know how it is one thing leads to another, and then you just decide to stay in because you want to be alone all night. After I tell her that, I think to myself how stupid that sounded.

Paxy, are you sure everything is okay with you and Joey this morning? You look a bit flustered and somewhat pale.

Jillie, everything is fine. I will be in my office this morning doing paperwork getting ready for our summer audit that is coming up. Then this afternoon Charlotte Dalecki will be here to look at what we are thinking about for the compound. Please get everything set up for her to see. Of course we want her to be impressed, and to purchase the pieces that we suggest. Stage the paintings that we have picked out for her to consider, and saved in the back room, then choose other art pieces in the gallery that you feel would look great with the paintings. Charlotte hosts many parties, and we want there to be as many pieces of art from the Brickstone as possible in her home, and for them to make a statement. Please make sure that the lighting on the show tables is adjusted perfectly, which will be so important for when she sees everything for the first time.

I will take care of everything, and let you know when she arrives.

Thank you Jillie, have I ever told you that you are the best, and I could not run the Brickstone without you?

Today has turned out to a wet and miserable day to be outside so working indoors all day will be perfect. Also, there is so much that I need to do that I am hoping to get my mind off of last night. Joey walks into my office at that very moment with a hot Latte for me. Wow, I thought that you would be too busy today working on the case to stop by much less bring me a Latte.

As it turns out, I am needed back at the scene of last night's shootings. So I wanted to tell you that I will probably not be back at all today, or tonight. I need to stay at the manor tonight. I also, want you to know that I have assigned another one of our undercover agents that you have not met yet, to watch your place all night. Just so that we can both be assured that you are safe. I have not had time yet to check out that black Lincoln.

I tell him, I don't really know how I feel about this. I would like to say that I don't feel that more security is necessary, but shit, I am afraid, so thank you.

Then after he leaves, I sit at my desk thinking of how I missed seeing any of these things coming, things that should have raised a red flag when they happened. Was I that desperate for something other than the Brickstone in my life, or for romance that was missing? Everything in my life now within just a short space of the last month has changed. I fall in love all over again, and with that comes such crazy complications. It all seems somehow so surreal. What could I be signing up for to have a life with Joey? Also, there is still the fact that we never seem to find the time to talk about if he will be going back to Washington when this case is over. I am sure that I will not be doing business again with Christos Artino, or Travis Gary. What will my life be like after this case is closed, do I just go back to just running the Brickstone like before this chaos began? Myranda has called three times this morning, and I have ignored her calls each time not knowing what to say, or not say. I decide maybe calling her back will somehow settle my nerves at least some.

Pax, have you heard about what happened last night out in San

Jose?

Yes, what did you hear?

My hell, something awful happened. I just spoke with Detective Zen Marlowe who told me that what they know for sure at this point in their investigation is that there were five border officers killed among the casualties of fifteen. Also, it looks like from the scene of where the crime took place that about four hundred rounds of ammo was used. The shooting lasted for only about thirty seconds according to neighbors that were questioned. But is sounded like a spray of machine guns opening up the earth.

Myranda, are you sure there was fifteen casualties, that is horrible.

That is what Zen told me. What is Joey saying? Zen said that it most definitely is part of a long time smuggling cartel that has plagued the Mexico-Arizona border for some years. Also, that the FBI has taken over the case for the most part, because they are getting closer to taking the Drug Lord himself down. You know he also, told me that Laura Pilner's case is somehow involved.

Did he say who they suspect the Drug Lord to be, or if he actually lives in Bisbee. Also, I am shocked to hear that Laura's case has anything to do with his. I would have never expected her to be involved with drugs. I used to see her in the early mornings jogging with her terrier, she would always smile and say good morning. She seemed so innocent.

I am pretty sure there are several people that are going to be surprised to hear about Laura, including our Mayor, unless he is a dirty politician, and is involved in some way himself. About the drug lord, I got the impression they do not know who it is exactly; however, he is suspected to be an American who yes might live in Bisbee, or near the border of Mexico, and works both sides. Paxy, I am sure this has something to do with why Joey is back in

Bisbee working undercover, so I thought that maybe you could give me more of the scoop so that I do not have to dig so hard in other places.

Myranda, if I knew something more to tell you about this I would. I get more information from you on the things that seem to be connected to Joey's undercover case than he himself would ever share with me.

Also, Myranda I have to ask, and I hate appearing to be so naïve, but what exactly is the position of a drug lord? You must deal all the time with those types of cases in your law office.

Well thank God, not very often. But what I do know is a drug lord seems to be the one in charge. Meaning the highest position there is in the entire drug cartel. He is responsible for supervising the entire drug industry in his purchased region of everything that happens. He appoints territorial leaders to work under him, they then make alliances and do the planning of high profile executions. Those executions right now are effecting our small community of Bisbee in a big way, I would say, and your man Joey is right in the middle of it all.

Well if this is all true, then it makes me feel even better about what he is doing to bring these assholes to justice.

Paxy, I just hope it all gets done sooner than later. I am truly afraid for you, and Joey's family if he is found out to be here working undercover with the FBI. Some of these drug dealers are ruthless, they will kill anyone that messes with their suppliers of drugs and guns. Zen said that it is also, bigger than just drugs and weapons, this cartel is suspected of billions of dollars in money laundering, and murder for hire.

Joey, has the Brickstone and my apartment being watched by one of the undercover agents for my safety. I am sure he has the manor being watched, also. He is staying there tonight, maybe he wants to talk to his family about why he is really here. He probably needs to tell them the truth after what happened last night, for their safety as well.

Paxy, please stay safe! You know if you are not comfortable at your apartment you can always stay with Sam and me.

Myranda, you are such a good friend, but I would never feel right about involving you and Sam in this. Besides, we both know that it would not take long for everyone in town to find out that I was staying at your home, and Joey says that it is important that everything in my life appears completely normal.

What about Jillie, what does she know?

Nothing much! Do you think that I should be worried about her safety too, maybe ask Joey for security for her, also?

Paxy, I think that we should both be worried right now about everything and everyone that these people may connect Joey to have a personal connection with, if he is found out. I am telling you they are not to be underestimated, they have no feelings for humanity.

Did Zen say that he was working with Joey?

No, of course not, he would never leak something like that, and compromise Joey, or anyone else.

I can hear Jillie and Charlotte Dalecki talking in the front part of the Gallery, so I tell Myranda that I have to go help Jillie with a client, then assure her that I will be safe, and that I will keep her posted as much as possible, then we hang up.

Chapter Eighteen

Charlotte seems to be a little on edge at first appearance, not quite herself. I wonder to myself if Joey has already talked to her and Frank. Of course knowing that it could just be the rain that is falling in sheets from the dark sky, with the low hovering clouds that are blanketing all of Bisbee. I love days like this; however, I know that it truly unnerves others. She is shaking, or maybe shivering, I can't tell if it is because she is upset, or cold from the rain.

Charlotte, can I have Jillie get you something hot to drink, you appear to be a little cold. I was just getting ready to have her make hot cinnamon tea for her and me.

Hot cinnamon tea sounds wonderful, if we are all going to enjoy a cup. I have had a dreadful beginning to my day. I almost had decided to cancel my appointment with you here today. Frank and Joey though both insisted that I get away from the manor, and keep my appointment with you.

I say to her, my heavens what happened to make your morning so dreadful?

I really am not sure what is happening. I was busy going through different rooms to make sure that the windows were all closed because it was raining so hard, when I heard Frank yelling and cursing at someone in the office. That someone ended up being Joey. I must have been in my bedroom getting dressed when Joey arrived, for I did not even know that he was back at the manor. He had said that he was going to be spending the entire evening with you, and that we should not expect him back before late today sometime. After realizing that it was Frank and Joey that were in the argument, I tried to intervene, neither would listen to me. It was quite obvious that they were arguing about something that had them both very upset and angry. The emotion that I witnessed in both of their voices this morning was a raw volatility towards each other. They practically both ordered me to leave, and keep our appointment. I have to tell you Paxton, I am sorry to say that I am not much in the mood right now to look at the art that you thought I might be interested in, I am so sorry.

Of course not, Charlotte. I completely understand that you would not be. That can always wait for a better time.

Paxton, did something happen while you and Joey were together last night to upset him?

Well, uhm….I don't think so. Did something happen that might have upset Frank?

I have no idea, he was at his weekly private poker game at the Turquoise Club House last night. It was late when he came in, and I was already asleep. But something horrible must of went down at that poker game last night for him to be like this this morning, unless it was Joey that brought bad news when he came in. Things were so bad that before I left this morning to come here I had to give the caretakers the Pacheco's the day off. The argument had gotten so explosive that I hated for the two of them to have to be there to witness it. I did not want them continuing to listen to the shameful shouting that was being spewed out between father and son. Paxton, in all of Joey's life I have never heard him disrespect, and say such horrible things like he was to his father this morning.

Charlotte, I can't imagine either of them behaving in such a manner towards each other, something is very wrong obviously. Do you think that Frank is pressuring Joey to leave Washington to come back to help with your family business? Joey did tell me that Frank's dream is that one day both Frank Jr. and Joey would take things over, and continue to build onto the empire that many generations of family have built.

No, not at this time. I have heard them many times speak of how important the job is that Joey does back in Washington, where he can keep an eye on the political powers and legislation that affects us, even here in Bisbee. They both feel that he is doing his part for the family business by being in Washington, at least for now. Having Frank Jr. be a part of the business does make Frank proud though, and one day when he is too old to do his part he will ask Joey to come back.

Paxton, dark days like this always make me nervous, and I have had a bad feeling all week. I think Frank sensed something was not right, also. Now that I think about it, he has been somewhat on edge all this past week. Maybe, it is all of Bisbee, things are just not right. Did you read in the newspaper, or hear about what happened last night in the San Jose neighborhood?

Yes, we did! It was horrible, Jillie and I were discussing that very thing earlier this morning.

When Mrs. Pacheco served my breakfast this morning she told me that she was talking with her daughter, who works for the Bisbee District Attorney's Office. She said that there were bloody mangled bodies found spread out all over the desert directly behind some of the homes in the San Jose. Mostly right now unidentified corpses that had been shot up so badly that it will take maybe up-to a month to identify some of them. The District Attorney, Larry Garcia said that apparently at least some of the shooters were using customized automatic weapons, judging from the amount of damage that was assessed. Also, they have fifteen people this morning at the mortuary, and it is almost impossible to determine at this time just how many shooters were involved, or how many more may have been wounded from the scattering of bullets fired. Apparently many of the roads plus a very large part of the desert is all taped off as a crime scene. Police officers, plus victim advocates from all over the county have been appointed to go from home to home today in that area. They are questioning everyone to find out if anyone may have seen something, and to make sure that innocent people in their own homes were not injured.

Jillie comes to the door of the office right then with our tea, and then asks if she can transfer a call back to me. I ask her if she would please take a message. She tells me that she tried to take a message, but the gentleman on the line insists on talking to me immediately. Charlotte and I share a quick glance of dread.

Miss Steele, this is Mr. Gary, please listen closely to what I am about to tell you. Agent Dalecki has asked me to pass this message on to you. He asked that you trust his word, and to do exactly as he requests. Things are about to change, and terrible things may happen very quickly. You need to leave the Brickstone with Mrs. Dalecki, Miss Townsend, and yourself immediately after hanging up the telephone from this call. If there are customers tell them that this call is from the fire department. They are getting ready to do a required drill that will take the rest of the day, and that there is no time they must evacuate immediately. Then do not lock the doors, turn out the lights, or turn on the alarms. Leave everything exactly as it is. Leave from your apartment upstairs using the fire stairs down to Howell Ave. Two DEA agents, along with their driver are in a Black Suburban waiting at the bottom of the staircase to take the three of you to safety, you can trust them. Miss Steele I must warn you that there is never a dress rehearsal in our line of work, just reality. You must leave now! We both hang up the telephone.

Paxton, what is it, Charlotte asks me.

Charlotte, Frank and Joey are fine, I hope. But no matter Joey just sent word that we need to leave the Brickstone immediately.

What on earth for, and to go where?

Jillie this includes you, also. Are there any customers still up front?

No, the last one left just as I was answering the telephone.

Okay ladies we have to all stay calm, but we must leave right now. We do not have time to talk about it, or anything else. You just need to trust me, and follow me upstairs where we will be leaving down the fire escape stairs from the back of my apartment. There is a car waiting for us.

Paxton, I demand to know what is going on before I go anywhere.

Charlotte, I do not have time to explain, or argue. Trust me though, you are putting all of us in grave danger if we do not freaking get the hell out of here right now.

The wind has picked up so now we have sideways sheets of rain. The metal grate staircase is slick, making it even more difficult to maneuver our way down the steep stairs. We are just getting to the Suburban that is waiting for us when two all black Lincoln Town Cars come onto Howell Ave. The first one drives around us, then the second one pulls up as close to our front bumper as possible without bumping us. Charlotte is already in the back seat, and I am pushing Jillie's shoulders to hurry her. We all get in the suburban safely; however, I can see that the Lincoln that went around us is now turned around, and coming up very close behind us. Nobody gets out of either of the Lincolns that have us blocked between them. The suburban windows light up with streaks of brilliant blue light, then the thunder rolls. The DEA agent in the front passenger seat barks with a voice of authority, guns ready. Now he is barking orders directed at the three of us to get as low as possible onto the floorboard. Charlotte, Jillie, nor I are saying anything at this point, only following orders. I could hear Charlotte's heart beating, and I was thinking, God do not let her have a heart attack, please! Then at that very moment I hear Jillie's voice in a barely audible whisper starting to pray. Another bark from the front seat telling us to stay low.

Ladies, no matter what you hear, or what happens stay low on the floor if you intend on staying alive.

We are now from what I can assess from the crouched down position that I have low on the floorboard trying to go forward, and ramming to push the car in front of us with great force. Bullets are now hitting our car, Charlotte begins to scream when one of the agents yells at her to shut up. I hear Jillie cry out that she has been hit. The bullets continue spraying directly at us. I can hear some of them ricocheting off of the car, and others that are causing breaking glass to spray all over us. There are sparks with streaks of fire from every direction, and the noise around us is deafening. I am trying to reach out to touch, or see Jillie without lifting my head. I cannot get my hand to her, but I can see blood coming from her mouth. Her eyes are open, but the life seems to be gone from them, they already look glassy, and she too is no longer screaming. Charlotte stopped screaming, and the look in her eyes tells me that she is probably gone into shock from terror.

Ladies hold on, we are going to make it out of here to get you to safety.

But, not for Jillie, I am thinking to myself. We hydroplaned on top of the high waters of the rain for a quick instant, before the driver gets control. Then the suburban tires are screeching as we are leaving upper Bisbee, with great force we are speeding on the curved road around the large open copper pit, going towards Lowell. Suddenly I feel my throat constrict, and then my stomach only hurts for a moment before I am puking violently. I can hear a voice on the suburban radio.

This is Chief Luna at Bisbee Police Headquarters, along with Agent FBI Dalecki. We need to know if all three of the passengers that are to be sequestered in your vehicle are with you, and safe?

This is DEA Agent Claus, our ETA is less than one minute. We have all three female passengers, one is down with a gunshot wound. I am not able to be sure of her condition. Please dispatch for an EMT Bus.

Have already done so, Agent Claus.

Agent Claus, this is now Agent Dalecki now on the radio. I need you to tell me which one of your passengers has been wounded.

Not sure, Agent Dalecki. Not even sure if she is alive. Just heard her scream that she had been hit, she is possibly just unconscious.

Chapter Nineteen

I wake up in a hospital bed, and can see that the large clock on the wall in front of me says 2:00 am. I can barely focus enough to see the woman in a police uniform looking out the window. I am groggy as if I have been drugged. I can hear other voices that are coming from outside the door.

The officer in my room turns to me to say: Ms. Steele, how are you feeling?

Kind of fuzzy, where am I? I realize that I can barely make out her name from the pin that is on her right shoulder, Cecilia Brock, Special Security Detail.

You are safe in a hospital in Sierra Vista, Arizona.

What?

You are safe, please try to remain calm.

Then I remember Jillie. Tears are forming in my eyes, where is

Charlotte Dalecki?

She was treated for shock after you all arrived, but is doing well, I am told. There are also, security guards with her.

Did Jillie have surgery too? Is she alright too? I need to talk to Agent Joseph Dalecki, please get him for me.

He was here around two hours ago to check on you, the doctor had just given you something for nausea, plus a sedative to help you sleep. He said to tell you that he would be back later this morning.

Please, help me remember yesterday, and last night. My memory is somewhat fuzzy, and I am having trouble focusing my eyes with my head hurting so badly.

Ms. Steele that does not surprise me you were involved in a terrifying situation that had to have caused you severe distress. When you arrived at the hospital, I was told that you were in a state of hysteria.

Please, just tell me. I have to know that my friend Jillie is okay.

Ms. Steele, I wish that I had some information to give to you; however, I was only given the details that are pertinent to my position in regards to your security. I do know though like I just told you Mrs. Dalecki is going to be fine. I have not heard anything regarding a Jillie.

You are assigned to my security? Does that mean that I am still in danger?

You do not need to worry about your safety there are two more officers that are posted right outside your door. No one, I mean no one will be able to get in here to harm you. Do you think that you could possibly sleep some more?

Probably not until I see Joey, and that was not an answer to my question.

Joey?

Yes, Agent Dalecki.

Oh, okay, well as I said he will be back to see you sometime this morning, probably soon. You really should get some more rest while you can before he gets here. Would you like me to call in a nurse for you?

I yell at her. I do not want to rest, I also, do not want a nurse. I just want know exactly what happened, and if my assistant, and dear friend is dead, or alive dammit. The only thing that I can remember is that we were under bullet fire and, she was hit by a bullet. I also, want to know who the hell was shooting at us. So do not freaking tell me what I need right now, or tell me to sleep. Instead, maybe you can at least find out if Frank Dalecki, Agent Dalecki's father is he here at the hospital with his wife, Charlotte? If so I need to talk to him.

I am not sure of who all has been contacted at this point. Let me see what I can find out for you.

Thank you! I am sorry to be this way, but my whole life has been turned upside down, and I want, no I need someone to tell me exactly what is happening.

Ms. Steele of course I understand that, but please try to understand where I am coming from, too. Right now my only priority is to keep you safe. By making sure that nothing happens to you it means that all of your questions can be answered in time, but only if you are alive. The one thing that I can share with you, is that the people that tried to kill you, or have you killed yesterday are very dangerous. It is also, believed that a Mr. Garza who is part of a Mexican/Arizona Cartel network was supposedly behind this. If that turns out to be true he is someone who the Mexican Police, Mexico/Arizona Border Patrol, and the United States FBI have been trying to flush out for decades. He is a ruthless Drug Lord to the core as any human being has ever been, along with the others that he works with.

Officer Brock, does anyone have any idea of who this drug lord's connections are in Bisbee.

Not to my knowledge, but of course that is a completely different department than mine. The one thing though that is widely known in every department. Is the "Code of Silence" that all cartels live by is almost impossible to break. Until someone that is getting up in years, and about to die, or is terminally ill, and wants to ease their conscious by finding God, only then are they willing to talk. The reason they will not talk before this is that you can never again regain any trust from the cartel. So you must be made as an example to everyone, even if you are family. This means the most wretchedness, excruciating, psychological, and physical pain that leads to a slow death that can ever be brought onto a human being.

I understand that you are just doing your job, and I am very scared of everything right now, so I will do exactly as you ask. I am also, afraid though for Mr. and Mrs. Dalecki's safety.

Ms. Steele knowing what I know about the signed orders from FBI Agent Joseph Dalecki to our Special Security Department regarding your safety. There are absolutely no doubts in my mind what so ever that his parents are under the same security as you. We are the best there is at what we do, I promise.

It is now 6:45 am, Joey walks in my room with a beautiful Tiffany Crystal Vase filled with incredible wildflowers. He puts the vase on the stand near my hospital bed, and tells officer Brock to please leave us alone for a few minutes. He tell her that her relief officer will be here at 7:00 am, so to please wait with the two guards that are outside my door until then. They are waiting for their day replacements, also.

She gives me a quick smile and wink, then tells me to stay strong. After the door closes behind her, Joey leans down close to my face to give me a light sweet kiss, and whispers, I will always make sure that you are safe so that I can keep coming back for more of this. I begin to cry, he holds me tight to let me just cry.

The flower vase is from the Brickstone. I borrowed two of them to put the flowers in that I picked myself from the garden at the compound. One for you, and one for my mother. I also, locked the Brickstone, set the alarm, and also put a nice notecard on the door, saying that you are closed for one week due to the storm last evening for repairs. I just left out the part that it was a shit storm caused by your boyfriend……By the way, nothing happened to the Brickstone!

Chapter Twenty

It feels so nice to be back in my apartment, even if I was only away from it for three days. There is still around the clock security guards in and around the Brickstone, and my apartment. I am assured though by Joey that it is only for a few more days until he is positive that the trouble and danger is over. Myranda has been by my side every day that I was in the hospital, and I am sure today will be no different. Joey called to see if I am up to him staying with me tonight. I asked him to give me some time, maybe just a few days to sort some things out in my mind. Myranda as expected arrives with some unexpected lunch, tacos from the El Charro.

Paxy, I am worried about you. Remember along time back when you asked me if I thought Joey might ever come back to Bisbee to work for his family business?

Yes, I think so, why?

Well he came back, maybe not to work with his family, but look at everything that has happened. I hate to say, or even think this, but I have a sick feeling that this could be a regular kind of thing in Joey's life as an agent. I also, do not see you fitting into that world.

I know. Joey asked if he could stay with me tonight. I asked him to give me some needed time to think about things, exactly the same things that have you concerned. I'm not sure that I fit in his world either. But, one thing that I did see for sure about him while I was in the hospital, is that Joey's job, the FBI Agent, seems to fit him like his own skin.

Paxy, he belongs in Washington, and not Bisbee. You, my friend, belong here at the Brickstone that you have worked so hard for, and love so much. Besides, I do not know what I would do if you ever left.

Six Days Later ...

Joey and I are sitting on my couch. Damn it, Joey. Damn you! No one has ever been able to make me so angry, then calm me down the way that you have always been able to do. You ruffle me up, then smooth me down in a matter of seconds, it is completely unnerving. You are going back to Washington to your career where you belong, and I have to protect myself. I have given everything a lot of thought this past week. I do not want to be a part of the world that you live in. I came back to Bisbee to live out a simple dream.

I love you, Paxton Steele! I plan on fighting for you. I also, plan to come back to Bisbee one day where I can live out a different dream of mine, and when I do, I want it to be with you. Right now though you are completely right, I do need to be in Washington, my work there is more important than you can know.

Joey, I know how important your work is. It's the part that it is more important than I am to you that I do not understand. Meaning, I just wish that you would tell me more about your work, and especially why it brought you to Bisbee. I still have so many questions that I need answered before I can move past what has happened here in the last several weeks. It was so hard trying to explain something that I did not really understand myself to Jillie's family when they came for her body. I know that the FBI explained what they could, but to a grieving family, that was not very much. They did appreciate the caring attitude that you, and the FBI had, it was also, nice that they paid for everything up to, and including her service. But, she had become like a loved little sister to me, and I want more answers just as they do. Joey, I am hurting, and I do not know if I can ever be the same again without those answers.

Paxton, I do not have answers to give you right now. You are just going to have to trust me.

Well Joseph, that seems to be the problem we have. Now yelling at him, I do not trust you, and I also, do not trust your family.

He yells back, why in the hell are you saying this, you have no reason to say this.

Don't I? You are keeping something big from me, and I am pretty sure that your family knows everything. But, I am an outsider to the almighty Dalecki family, so that to you means you cannot trust me.

You are acting irrational!

Maybe so, but it is what I believe. Joey, I think you need to leave.

I will leave now, and I will be driving back to Washington in two days. Please come have dinner at the manor with myself, and my family tomorrow night. I will have my mother call you with a time. I have to see you at least for that short time before I leave.

Please, if you have ever loved me you will come have dinner with us, for me.

Joey, no promises, please leave.

I decide to go to the manor to have dinner with the Dalecki's. Besides, I cannot bear to not see Joey before he leaves. What if I never see him again?

After Dinner at the Dalecki Manor

Paxton, I am so pleased that you were able to join our entire family tonight for dinner before Joey leaves, after all who knows when he will be back again. Also honey, I pray for us that we will be able to forget, and forgive this awful thing that we experienced, and lived through together.

Thank you Charlotte, and yes who knows when he will be back?

Paxton, we are going to say goodnight now as we need to take the twins home. Also, Joseph my brother you take good care of yourself back in Washington. I look forward to talking again soon, says Frank.

Joey and I enjoy a nighttime tradition with his parents of a short glass of Brandy. They then excuse themselves for the evening.

Paxton, I want to talk to you alone before you leave, please will you join me in my father's office? It is where we will have the most privacy.

I only have a short time, tomorrow is opening day again at the Brickstone. So, I want to get home to bed.

Good, I am happy to hear that your plans are to re-open tomorrow.

Once in the office, we just stand there, seems that both of us do not know what to say.

"There's always a moment that separates the past from the future, and that moment is now"

By: Aniekee Tochukwu Ezekiel

This is the quote that is running through my mind as I look at Joey this very moment. His demeanor seems to give the sense that he is at a loss for what to do next.

Joey, let's just say goodbye for now.

Paxy, I love you!

Joey, how can you love someone that you do not trust?

I trust you Paxy, there are just things that are too dangerous right now for me to share with you.

That excuse of being too dangerous for me to know, no longer holds water with me. I have a right to know everything after the way you, and the entire damn FBI used me. Just you telling me that you love me is not enough, without you telling me the whole story of what comes with me loving you back.

Now he has nothing to say, he just starts to circle me like a wolf that is assessing his desert.

Very well Paxy, let's forget about love for the moment. What about the passion we have for each other?

What about it? I ask this as he is slipping behind me. He continues to watch me carefully while he is coming back around from behind me, like some kind of wolf predator I think to myself.

If love does not play into how you feel about me, then I ask you where our passion falls. Do you think that you can be satisfied with a life without the passion you and I have found? It sounds like a pretty boring and loveless life to me.

I have the Brickstone, which is the only passion I need.

Paxy, I know you better than that, you want more.

I look straight into his eyes now, and he is only a breath away from me. Not true, it is all I had before you came back, and I was very content.

Content, there is a good word.

He is almost laughing before saying, I don't believe you. Our love, our passion, our throwing it all away would haunt you if we give up on what we have found again together.

Joey, I am sorry, but right now our love and passion are just no longer that important to me.

Paxy, you may say, and even think that is true right now, or you may not want it to be important, but it is.

With his gaze right on my face, and so serious he lifted one hand to run his thumb over the pounding pulse in my throat.

Joseph, I plan on proving to you just how unimportant it is to me. I have lost that craving that I had for us.

I doubt that he says as he starts backing me up against the fireplace. So the way you trembled with passion in my arms the last night that we made love, meant nothing to you, and is now gone?

My back is as far up against the stones on the fireplace as it can go, and he is tempting me with short tender teasing kisses on my neck, then up to my mouth.

I am already beginning to weaken, and damn him to hell, he senses it. He slips both hands around my waist, pulls me up against him. It means something, when every time we are together we ignite.

We do not ignite, I whisper in his ear with my voice quivering, and my entire body now on fire. His kisses are still tender, but longer, and deeper on my mouth. He is so gently teasing my bottom lip with tiny bites, and suckles. All of this, and he is now fondling my breast through the linen top that I wore tonight. This catches me by some surprise, so I gasp just a little before I hear my self-moan, and lean into his seductive touch. As I enjoy him caressing me again, I feel that liquid heat swirl in my belly that I have felt with him so many times before in the last several weeks.

Paxy, I am not sure, but you certainly feel passionate, and about to ignite to me. He looks up at me, and kisses my cheek, then lets his mouth slowly come all the way down my jaw, and to my throat. I hate giving in, but my body is aching for him.

Sweet torture isn't it, he says?

I manage to pull back just far enough to whisper, no torture is what I have been living with lately Joey, everything being so secretive. You my best friend not trusting me enough to let me into your world so that I can understand your soul. Maybe, this is just my way of torturing you, for a change.

Well Paxy, I must say it is working.

He moves my hand to the crotch of his jeans, and our kisses become even thirstier for each other. We make our way to red leather sofa where he straddles my body. He pulls my top up over my arms, then my skirt down, and off. His pants are next to come off.

I want us to feel this passion we have for one another baby doll, just let it happen.

He gives a soft moan as he delves his hard sex into me. We are both writhing with pleasure, my heart feels like it could come right out of my chest. We continue to thrust up and down until we relinquish our hot juices at the very same moment to each other.

You are still so warm and wet, and so beautiful. I want to take you again. Then with his sensuous moves he is causing my entire body to quake, as he takes me yet again with our bodies melting into one. He whispers in my ear, Paxy give yourself to the rhythm of our naked bodies, and feel our dance of love. We do love each other.

I at that moment think, but is love always enough?

Epilogue

Right now, today, Joey is in Washington, and I am in Bisbee. Myranda and I have just returned from the trip to Rome, where I completed the job that I started for Joey and Christos. It was very successful, and I am sure that the paintings will be back with the owners very soon, if Christos has anything to say about it.

I have always known that there are no guarantees that Joey and I will ever come full circle with a life together, because there are just no guarantees in life. We stay in touch as much as our busy schedules and separate lives allow. I heard the other day at the Brickstone, that the grape vine at the Dalecki Manor, has it that Joey does spend time with a woman from Annapolis, Maryland. She is a Real Estate Attorney named Johnna Hannah.

I have not yet begun my search for another assistant as I know there will never be another Jillie. Also, I am learning to live my life by another plan called, Plan B.

Plan A: was always the first choice. You know, the one where everything works out to be happy ever after. But more often than not, you find yourself dealing with the upside-down, inside-out version, where nothing goes as it was supposed to. It was at this point that the real test of my character came in to play….Do I sink, or swim? Do I wallow in self-pity, and play the victim, or simply shift gears, and make the best of one of life's unexpected happenings. The choice is mine to make. After all….Life is all about Plan B

I am enjoying my dream with the Brickstone in this quirky, and busy little community called Bisbee. Plus, I think Joey's passion for me may just haunt him until he comes back to live out his dream.

The End

About The Author

Laticia Waggoner was born in the incredible Rocky Mountains of Colorado in 1957 then grew up in Bisbee Arizona which is in the beautiful Mule Mountains....She was married young and as fate would have it she returned to Colorado. She and her husband raised three amazing children Travis, Casey, and Johnna whom all have beautiful and amazing families of their own. Her husband John Proctor sadly passed away in 2010. Laticia had always shared with him that one day she would like to write a book, or books. He encouraged her to believe in that dream, and he always believed she would.

So in a new chapter of Laticia's life this is her first fictitious mystery romance, and the first book in a short story series of "Joesph Dalecki and Paxton Steele " Hope you enjoy reading this as much as she enjoyed breathing the life into it.....

Made in the USA
Columbia, SC
21 July 2021